Goose Island

written by Lucinda J. Davis

copyright 2018

D1553064

This book is dedicated to my dog Honey who was my faithful companion for 18 years and never complained once. She remains in my heart forever.

A special thanks to Char Reed for her time and knowledge

cover by Alysha Reszke
A Bushel & A Peck Photography

Prologue

The tires screeched on the pavement. There was no time for reaction. The husband and wife didn't get any last words to each other. No time for I love you's. No goodbyes. The impact was so sudden the only thoughts they had were of death.

When her car struck theirs they watched the glass shatter and although it happened in seconds it seemed like it was in slow motion. The cars didn't stop immediately when they hit. Once they struck, the couples car tumbled and rolled out of control. The female's car continued until it ran into a tree.

The wife could feel her teeth crumble in her mouth. She was conscious the entire time and she wondered if she survived how bad would this be. Would she be paralyzed, have broken bones, or get impaled?

Her eyes were shut, possibly from the airbags. But she couldn't feel the impact of the bags when they deployed. There were too many other things going on.

As the car tumbled she screamed, but she didn't hear her own voice. She didn't hear anything. She felt dirt and debris hitting her face and body. Chunks of glass and metal spun around in the car like a giant tumble dryer. The debris sliced her skin. Then her leg snapped and she screamed louder but still didn't hear herself. When they finally stopped rolling because the car hit something unmovable, there was one final snap and she stopped screaming.

The husband was not conscious but alive. The fire truck's lights danced together with the police car's lights, waiting for the ambulance to arrive. The smoke filled the air providing the atmosphere for the dancing lights. It looked like a war zone and death was there, but the scene made everyone else feel alive.

Gawking drivers rolled by slowly. Their cars drove over the broken pieces of glass making a crunching noise on the pavement.

The man's eyeglasses lay broken on the mangled dashboard dripping with blood. The firemen worked diligently to pull the man from the car because he was still breathing. They loaded him into the ambulance and drove away. He would linger for days, but he would never say goodbye.

The female that was texting while driving was shaking and crying, but she only cut her hand.

Goose Island

Chapter One

Today was one of those days when the clock didn't seem to move. Joy was restless at her desk again. Her cubicle was confining. It was a space that would make any normal person feel claustrophobic. She moved her chair slightly one way and it banged into the wall. She moved the chair a bit the other way and it banged into the desk. She was short but still there was no leg room.

She used to have a bigger office space that was more open. The corporate beasts decided it was more important to utilize every ounce of space, because they didn't care about the comfort of their employees.

Even though she worked with a lot of people she felt very lonely at her job. She didn't have much social interaction during her eight hour work day. Her days consisted of staring at a computer screen and occasionally speaking on the phone to some rather mean people and some perverts too. The last call she took today went something like this, "Hello, this is Joy how can I help you today?"

Male caller said, "I don't know, why don't you tell me how you can help me, Joy" in a sensual tone. Only Joy didn't think it was sensual at all she was just disgusted.

Joy responded professionally, "Well sir, you called me and if you aren't going to tell me the purpose of your call then I do have to end this conversation."

The male caller replied in a creepy voice, "Oh well little girl why don't you stop by my house and I'll give you some candy."

Joy told him, "I'm sorry sir, but it appears I can't help you today so have a pleasant day. Goodbye." She rolled her eyes and as she hung up the phone the man started to swear at her and use vulgar profanity. It seemed to be his hobby or how he got his kicks.

If it wasn't the perverts calling in it was high strung women screaming or aggressive men barking at her. She tolerated this type of verbal abuse on a fairly regular basis, just because her job required her to take phone calls. She also knew these people must have some serious issues, so she remained as nice as she possibly could when dealing with angry individuals.

Joy often thought about how easy it was for people to be rude to someone on the phone. It's easy to forget there is a real human being on the other end. She dealt with all types of people and would catch them at their worst behavior. Even clergymen would call and she would catch them in lies. That didn't help her faith in times like these. She was growing tired of being everyone's door mat and she didn't feel appreciated.

She never enjoyed taking part in office gossip, so she kept to herself. This action alone made her a target of the gossip. Many people would speculate why she would stay to herself. She just didn't care. Joy was there for a paycheck plain and simple. She had attempted to be friends with some of her co-workers but they all just wanted to talk about work and each other.

Today her head ached, she didn't know if she was getting a sinus infection, a brain tumor, or if she was just working too much. She couldn't focus on the tasks in front of her. She just wanted to go home but she had used up all of her vacation time and sick leave on other days like this. Today she found every reason she could to get away from her desk and try to make time move faster.

When she was at her desk, Joy would doodle little drawings to make time pass by. Today she was drawing simple little spirals and triangular shapes. Some days she would draw flowers or just scribbles. Walking around in the office during moments like these seemed to help a little too. She was uncomfortable in her own skin today. She kept looking at the lottery ticket she had bought this morning when she was on her way to work. She kept hoping she would win so she could go somewhere, anywhere, just away from here. She knew chances were slim but it doesn't hurt to dream, does it?

Joy had already wandered over to the coffee pot at least eight times today and it was only half past two. A few times she went to the coffee pot just to top off her cup because it was nearly full to the brim anyhow. She had gone to the bathroom as many times as she dare. She thought people might start suspecting she had a bladder infection or worse, but who really wants to hang out in a smelly restroom all day? Of course, sometimes the smells that drifted into her cubicle were just as bad as being in the restroom. She could swear one co-worker would intentionally fart every time he walked by *her* cubicle.

At about three o'clock she strolled out into the stairwell where there was a window she liked to gaze out as often as possible. Many days she would step into the stairwell and contemplate her life. She would wonder how her life could be better if she would just make some changes. However, Joy was afraid of change. It had been her experience that change was difficult. Most of the time change was not welcome in Joy's life.

She stood at the window on the second floor looking out over the fire station next door. The flag over the station waved brilliantly in the wind. She was glad to see it flying high since it seemed to be half mast more often than not.

It had already snowed about six inches and the large fluffy flakes were still coming down. She fixated on a snowflake and watched it fall all the way to the ground. She got lost in the beauty of each flake but also saw the flip side to them. She thought, "it was such a nasty drive in today, I'm sure it will be treacherous on the way home." Joy dreaded the commute to and from work nearly as much as she hated her job. She struggled not to think about either since she believed she needed to try to focus on the positive.

A little brown squirrel was playing in the snow and it darted back and forth then ran up the tree where it found a branch to stop and look back at Joy. She smiled as she watched him nibble on something. The little squirrel would look up at her and twitch his nose and then go right back to his afternoon snack.

A fire truck pulled into the station and caught her attention. She began watching the traffic outside. A few cars went sliding by in the slippery city streets. The tree where the squirrel sat somewhat blocked her view, but she could see pretty well through the branches. She was looking at the road by the fire station and noticed the street lights. She watched the lights as they changed from green to yellow and then to red. The lights entertained her as they swayed in the wind.

Then she noticed a city bus with the words "Goose Island" printed on the side in some type of advertisement. She began to remember her college days and how her friends called her "Goose". She never did find out why they called her that but she assumed it had something to do with a night of drinking that she would rather forget.

Joy wasn't sure what the ad on the bus was advertising, but she began to daydream a bit. She began to think how Goose Island sounded like a nice place to be and since Goose had been her nickname it could be her place, just hers alone. She wondered what kind of place Goose Island would be, tropical or maybe just a foggy refreshing foreign place where the people wore raincoats sometimes. Of course, right now any place would be a nicer place to be. She would rather be just about anywhere other than her tight cubicle which felt like a small prison and sometimes the torture was just the voices of her coworkers prattling on about nothing all day.

She looked at her watch and noticed about fifteen minutes had passed by so she scurried back to her desk. No one had noticed she was gone, in fact she was beginning to feel invisible. She hadn't dated anyone in several months, in fact it would soon be a year.

People at work didn't notice her much and if she spoke up it was as if no one even heard her. People would talk over her and completely ignore what she said. Some days she thought she might not even exist. Most of the time it didn't bother her.

The last time a coworker responded to something she said, it was the new girl, Olivia. She introduced herself to Joy, "Hi, I'm Olivia. How are you?"

Joy responded honestly, "I don't feel very well. I think it's this place, but it's nice to meet you. I'm Joy."

Olivia scoffed sharply and sneered, "Joy is it? Well, you don't seem very *joyful* now do you?" as she turned away to speak to someone else nearby. Unfortunately, this was not the first time someone had said these words to her. She recalled several coworkers, a boyfriend and even her own Mother mockingly telling her she wasn't a joyful person. Some days it was just tough being named Joy.

Joy came back from the stairwell, sat down in her chair, and began typing. It was a slow day and the phone hadn't been ringing all afternoon. It was difficult to concentrate on her job. The office loudmouth had been running full blast today and always about much of nothing. Joy thought she must just like to hear herself talk. She talked so much that Joy didn't know how she got any work done. It actually seemed like the company was paying the office loudmouth to talk all day. Joy didn't mean to eavesdrop but it was impossible not to listen due to the volume of her voice.

Paul had just left the desk of the loudmouth after a ten minute conversation about what was on television last night. Then Olivia came over to talk to her. It seemed like there was always someone at the loudmouth's desk. If there wasn't she would just holler over the wall to anyone that would listen.

"I had a hamburger for lunch today. It was so big I had to eat it with a fork," Olivia said.

"If it's that big it's pretty big!" replied loudmouth, "and I should know, I've got a BIG mouth!"

Joy rolled her eyes and nodded but no one saw, she was in her cubicle. She began to have thoughts about the ad on the bus again. Those words "Goose Island" were lingering in her mind like a fresh breeze. Her mind began to drift, she felt a little dizzy, and suddenly she found herself laying washed up on a pebble filled beach.

It was a cool and cloudy day and she was drenched and shivering in her clothes. She didn't know how she got here and was completely confused. She looked to her right and then to her left. She was next to a dock. She didn't know what to think when she looked up and saw an elderly man and woman rushing towards her. The man yelled, "Joy!" as they reached down and lifted her soggy body from the shore and wrapped her in a blanket. Pebbles and sand stuck to her clothing and she could feel the sand inside her clothes.

Joy asked, "Where am I? How do you know me? Who are you?"

The elderly man was wearing khaki pants and a plaid shirt and a yellow raincoat. He had a full head of gray hair, a kind round face, and a bit of a pot belly. She was still trying to focus and things were a bit blurry but she could see his name tag on his shirt. His name was David.

The couple held Joy between them as they began to help her walk away from the water towards their vehicle.

She asked him again, "David, where am I? How do you know me? How did I get here?"

David answered, "Well now see, you know who I am. You've already answered one question on your own. He looked at his wife and said, "Patricia, poor thing must have bumped her head." His false teeth flopped a little loosely in his mouth as he spoke.

"No, I don't know you. You are wearing a name tag, David" Joy said frantically as she tried to get some real answers.

"Yes, David you ARE wearing your name tag," Patricia added as she nodded and smiled. Patricia looked at Joy with compassion and told her, "Let's get you home and warm you up. I'll make a pot of tea and we'll talk about everything, dear."

Patricia looked like a goodhearted woman probably in her sixties. She was a plump woman with short curly gray hair and glasses. She was wearing a blue floral dress, a navy blue raincoat, and white nurses shoes.

David opened the door of the SUV and they boosted Joy into the backseat. David and Patricia got in the front and looked back at Joy. They both smiled at her.

"We sure are glad we found you when we did. You could have drowned," Patricia told her.

David started the vehicle and pulled out of the parking lot. As they turned onto the road she saw a sign "Welcome to Goose Island". Joy gasped as her heart began to beat rapidly. Then she felt faint and passed out in the back seat.

She was startled when someone said, "Joy, aren't you going home? It's five o'clock!" She was back at her desk in the real world and all she could think is that she dozed off. Her heart was still racing, but she thought it was caused by her co-worker waking her up. She was completely baffled at how real her daydream was. She remembered feeling wet and cold and everything was so vivid. She actually felt a little damp all over. "Maybe I'm coming down with the flu, I must have been sweating." she thought.

She gathered her belongings and left the building. As she labored to walk through the heavy snow to her car she just couldn't get Goose Island out of her mind. She began cleaning the snow off her car and another coworker Paul pulled up in his gas guzzling jacked up pickup truck. "Hey Joy, are you stuck?" he yelled over his loud engine.

"No, I don't think so…." Joy began timidly.

"Well that's good," said Paul.

"…but if you'd like to stick around for a minute…" Joy turned around to see Paul speeding away.

14

Still she managed to get her rusty old car started and drive home through the deep snow and slick roads. It was a white knuckle drive, people were driving too fast and even trying to pass on the snow covered icy roads. Today it took her an hour and a half to get home. On a good day the drive only took thirty minutes.

Joy lived alone in a small two bedroom home with her cat named Fitch and her two goldfish, Splish and Splash. Fitch was an orange tabby she found in a peach box in an alley. The peach box said "Fitch Peaches", so she named her Fitch.

Fitch came to greet her at the door because she was hungry and ready to be fed. She looked at Joy as if to tell her, "you're late!" Joy grabbed the scoop for the cat food and filled Fitch's dish, while she asked the cat how her day was. Naturally, the cat didn't answer it just buried it's head in the bowl of food and gobbled it down. Then she walked over to the aquarium and told her fish about the strange thing that happened today. She was trying to sort it all out.

Feeding her fish reminded her of the smells when she was on Goose Island. "I could actually smell the fish in the air and taste the salt water in my mouth," she told her fish. After a while, she decided it was just her vivid imagination and she went to bed early.

15

Chapter Two

The alarm clock buzzed and Joy hit the snooze button several times, she didn't want to go to work. After thirty minutes of hitting the snooze button Fitch came and sat on her head.

Joy opened one eye squinting at Fitch, "are you telling me it's time to get up?" Fitch put her paw on Joy's face and Joy smiled.

She finally dragged herself out of bed yawning and rubbing her eyes. It was just another ordinary day. She went through her morning routine and everything went well.

Her commute to work was uneventful as usual, except for the jerk beeping, rushing past her, and flipping her off because she sat at a green light a little too long. Her thoughts were elsewhere, but she was dreading work again.

As she walked into the office the receptionist Sarah said her usual "good morning" and Joy told her the same. Joy sat down at her desk and logged into her computer at 8am. She thought, "oh I forgot to fill my coffee cup". So, she took her coffee cup to the kitchen area and filled it.

There was a window in the kitchen and it just so happened while she was filling her cup she saw the city bus drive by again with the ad for "Goose Island". Everything that had happened yesterday came rushing back to her. She went back to her desk and tried to work but just couldn't. She took a sip of her coffee and became dizzy again.

The next thing she knew she was waking up in a bedroom. She was tucked in bed all cozy under a beautiful handmade quilt. She knew this wasn't her bed. The room looked like it belonged to an elderly person. The flowered wall paper was really out dated. There were silly little nick-knacks all over the room. Whoever lived there seemed to like strawberries and gnomes. There was a pink rotary dial phone on the nightstand next to her. She thought, "Wow, who even uses those things anymore? I wonder if it even works?!"

She picked up the hand piece and put it to her ear. Someone was having a conversation. She heard a man talking and then Patricia said, "just a minute...I think someone picked up the other line. I'll call you back, dear." The man said, "okay, bye" and the phone went click.

Joy hung up quickly when she heard footsteps coming toward the bedroom. She laid her head on the pillow pretending she was sleeping. The door creaked open slowly and she heard Patricia say, "Joooy, are you up?" in a quiet voice.

Joy moved a bit as if she were just waking up. She squinted her eyes and yawned and said, "how did I get here?"

Patricia said, "David and I brought you back to our house. You passed out in the car. We think you may have bumped your head down at the docks, so we had the doctor take a look at you. He said you'll be fine. He thinks you just lost your balance and fell into the water. What were you doing out in Thunder Bay by yourself anyhow? You know the waters are choppy this time of year."

Joy didn't want to alarm Patricia so she didn't tell her she was sitting at her desk and now she's in her bed.

Instead, she just said, "Look, I don't know who you are and I don't know how you know who I am. I've never seen you before in my life! I never heard of Goose

Island until yesterday. In fact, nothing here looks familiar!"

"Oh dear, you must have hit your head harder than the doctor thought. I will get the doctor back over here to have a look. I think you might have amnesia!" said Patricia.

Patricia picked up the pink rotary phone and called the doctor, "Dr. Lewis, Joy is awake and I think you need to come take another look at her. She doesn't remember me. I'm very concerned…..okay we'll see you soon. Bye."

Joy got a little worried, she actually felt fine now. Her headache was gone and she didn't feel dizzy. She was feeling pretty good. "Patricia, I'm really okay. I feel good. I don't need a doctor," Joy told her.

"No, you ARE NOT fine!," Patricia persisted, "You WILL see the doctor, so just lay there and I'll get you a cup of tea. I have dinner in the oven and I need to go check on that too. I'll be right back. You just holler if you need anything."

Joy thought, "Dinner? I just had breakfast."

Joy's anxiety was kicking in, and she started to wonder what if the doctor found something wrong with her? What if she couldn't get back to the real world? What if her her cat and fish starve? what if, what if, what if…?!

She couldn't even get a grasp on time. But she knew something strange was happening, she just didn't know what. She tried to wake herself up by pinching her arm and slapping herself in the face. It was useless, she didn't know how she got there and she didn't know how to get back home.

Patricia walked into the room with a tray in her hands. The tray had a silver teapot, a china tea cup, some toast, jams, honey, and of course some strawberries.

Patricia waddled over next to the bed, "Look I made you a little snack to go with your tea and these strawberries were picked fresh today from my garden. They are so sweet and delicious, I'm sure you'll love them. You need to get a little food in your tummy and get your strength back. You haven't eaten in well over a day."

Joy tasted a strawberry while Patricia poured her tea. It was delicious, probably the best strawberry Joy had ever tasted.

"Mmmmmm, I can't believe how sweet these strawberries are! You grew these yourself?" Joy sipped some tea.

Patricia looked at Joy surprised and said, "Joy, now you know you helped plant those strawberries. You really don't remember, do you?"

Joy put her head down, she felt ashamed she couldn't remember. She really felt bad because this woman was treating her so kind.

Just then the door bell rang. "Oh that must be Dr. Lewis!" Patricia hurried to the door. "Come in, come in, Dr. Lewis. Right this way," she led him down the hall to the bedroom at the end.

Joy was surprised when she saw Dr. Lewis, he was a handsome young man with well-defined facial features. He had blonde wavy hair and nice tan skin. He smiled and his teeth sparkled. His baby blue eyes topped it all off. He wasn't at all what she was expecting. She thought he would be an older wrinkled man like her doctor in the real world. He acted like he knew her well.

"Joy, so what is this you are telling Patricia you don't know her?" Dr. Lewis asked.

Joy looked downward again, "Yes, I only just met her the other day on the beach with David."

"Oh, so you remember, David?" he asked.

"Well, I remember him from the other day, but I only just met him too," she said.

"And do you remember me?" the doctor asked.

"No," she said, "I don't know where I am, who you are, or what is happening."

21

The doctor listened to her heart and he looked in her ears. He checked her eyes, nose and reflexes. He took her temperature and blood pressure. He did all of the usual stuff that doctors do. Then said, "I'm going to have to run a few tests, but I'm quite sure she has amnesia and it's difficult to say if her memory will come back at this point. I won't know anything until we get the test results back. For now I want you to rest and try to remember your life. I'll see you tomorrow in my office."

Joy said, "Okay, doctor I'll see you tomorrow."

Joy wondered if she would even be there tomorrow or would she be back in her real life. After all, as far as she knew this was all just her imagination. She did want to see the handsome doctor again. So, she decided even if she made it back to her real life she would try to get back to Goose Island to see him.

Patricia walked Dr. Lewis to the door, Joy couldn't hear what they were saying but she heard them say their goodbyes and Patricia shut the door. Patricia came back to the bedroom and told Joy, "Dinner will be ready soon and David will be home from work. If you have enough strength we'd like you to join us at the table, but if you aren't feeling well I can bring your dinner in here."

Joy told her, "No, I think I'd like to come to the table for dinner. That would be nice."

"Okay, well your clothes have been washed and they are hanging in the closet," Patricia motioned to the left, "and if you want a shower, the bathroom is the first door on the right."

"I think I could use a shower," Joy answered.

Patricia left the room and Joy slid her legs over the side of the bed and stood up. She walked over to the mirror and thought, "well at least that is me in the mirror". She picked up a gnome off the dresser to look at it and set it back down and shrugged her shoulders. Then she walked to the closet and found her clothes and laid them out on the bed.

She went into the bathroom to take a shower. There were more strawberries and gnomes, they were even on the shower curtain. Joy turned on the water in the shower and tested it with her hand. She slipped off the nightgown that Patricia must have loaned her and stepped into the shower. The water felt good and she kept thinking any moment she would wake up and be back at her desk. She was sure her boss would be standing over her yelling at her for falling asleep on the job. But she finished her shower and dried off. She went back to the bedroom and got dressed. Her clothes felt softer. It was almost as if her imaginary world was more real than her real world.

Things tasted better, felt better, smelled better, and she felt more alive.

She heard David enter the house, "Patricia! I smell dinner and it smells fantastic! I can't wait to dig in!"

Joy walked out into the hallway and tip toed until she got to the kitchen. David saw her, "Well, there she is! You're looking well, Joy. How are you feeling?"

"Umm, good," she answered quietly.

Patricia chimed in, "She still doesn't remember us." Patricia was putting food on the table, steaming dishes of good home cooked food.

"Well, that's okay," David said, "I'm sure it's just temporary. She'll be back to normal in no time." Patricia shot David a quick glare. Joy didn't know why but assumed it was normal marital stuff.

"Have a seat and help yourself," Patricia told her.

David began loading up his plate and shoveling the food into his mouth. "Slow down, David. The food isn't going anywhere," Patricia scolded.

David coughed a bit trying to speak as he swallowed what was in his mouth, "Ahem, did you talk to Michael yet?" he asked Patricia.

"Yes, he called earlier today, but our call was interrupted. He will be home in just a few more days," she answered.

24

"Does he know?" David asked.

"We can talk about this later," Patricia said.

Joy's eyes darted back and forth between Patricia and David. She didn't know who Michael was or what they were talking about but it seemed like they were hiding something from her.

"Well, we need to prepare her for when he comes home," David told Patricia.

"Who is Michael and what does he have to do with me?" Joy asked them.

Patricia and David's eyes met and they knew they had to tell her something. "Joy, Michael is our son and your husband." David told her in a very serious tone of voice.

Joy was putting a glass up to her mouth to take a drink of water just when they told her. She froze, dropped the glass and it shattered all over the floor. Patricia jumped into action to clean up the mess.

"David, I told you we should discuss this later. You've shocked her. We could have waited until he got home and see if she remembered him," Patricia said as she scrubbed and grabbed pieces of glass.

David defended himself, "I'm sorry, Patricia, but wouldn't it be more of a shock for him to show up and we tell her then? I thought maybe we could jog her memory!"

Joy began apologizing for breaking the glass, "Here let me help you," she said as she got down on the floor to scoop up shards of glass.

"No, no, you'll hurt yourself just sit down," Patricia insisted.

"Ouch," Joy shouted as a piece of glass sliced her finger.

"See, I told you," Patricia said as she grabbed Joy's hand and led her to the sink to clean the blood.

"Oh I'm fine, it's just a little cut. It just needs a little bandage," Joy said.

"That doesn't look little, Joy," David said.

Patricia bandaged Joy's finger and everyone calmed down, except for Joy. Joy appeared to be calm on the outside but inside she was a bundle of nerves. Joy had a whole new set of questions in her mind. She was wondering what Michael was like and how all of this could be possible. Her head was spinning. She became dizzy and passed out again.

When she opened her eyes she was sitting at her desk back in the real world. She was very disoriented. She looked at the clock on her computer. The time read 9:04 am, and it was still the same day. The same as when she had logged in this morning. Not much time had passed at all, just about an hour maybe. She stood up and peeked around the office to see if anyone had noticed anything. Everything seemed fine.

She hadn't done any work yet and her coffee was cold. She decided she better start working before someone noticed. She didn't want to get in trouble. She started to type and then she saw it.

The bandage that Patricia had put on her finger was still on her finger and the blood was still fresh. Her finger was throbbing. She thought, "How could this be? What is happening to me?"

Chapter Three

Later that day, Joy decided to call her friend Nicole while she was taking her lunch break. Nicole didn't answer so she left her a message that she needed to get together and talk if she was free for dinner tonight. Then she called her other friend Julie.

"Hello?" Julie answered.

"Hi, Julie it's Joy. I need to talk to someone. I feel like I'm losing my mind. Can you meet at my house tonight, I'll make dinner."

"Sure, what's wrong?" Julie asked.

"I can't explain over the phone. I'm on my lunch break and there just isn't enough time," Joy said.

"Alright, I'll see you tonight. Do you want me to bring a bottle of wine or something?" Julie asked.

"No, no I probably shouldn't have any wine tonight, but thanks," Joy answered.

When Joy got home, she got a text message from Nicole confirming that she would also be coming for dinner. She put a pot of water on the stove and pulled pasta from a box. She tossed some spaghetti in the boiling water. She started cutting up vegetables and stopped to look at the cut on her finger. She wondered if she could have imagined it and just didn't remember hurting herself. She was having second thoughts about telling her best friends.

She thought about how many times she had forgotten things. She knew how easy it was to get caught up in her thoughts on the drive to or from work and not remember the drive at all. She had walked into a room countless times forgetting why she went in the room in the first place. And she knew this was normal for most people to forget things. She just knew she couldn't make excuses for cutting her finger and not remembering how she injured it or the fact that she bandaged it. She was pretty sure this was not normal.

There was a knock at the door. Joy opened the door, it was her friend Julie. "Come on in! I just put the spaghetti on to cook and dinner will be ready soon. I invited Nicole too. I need as much advice as possible."

"What's goin' on?" Julie asked curiously.

"Just wait, wait til Nicole gets here. It's so difficult to explain and I'm afraid you won't believe me when I tell you. I hardly believe it myself," she told her.

"Okay, well I have some news," said Julie. "Remember that guy I told you about, I met him a couple weeks ago?"

"You mean Eric?" Joy asked as she continued making dinner.

"Yes, we are really hitting it off! We've been out a few times and he's so sweet. Valentine's Day is coming up and he's taking me to dinner," Julie beamed as she spoke.

"Awww, well I'm really glad for you. I hope that works out. You're such a positive person and so pretty. You deserve a really good guy," said Joy.

"And you deserve a good guy too, Joy. You know you are a great person. I think Eric has a friend..." Julie started.

Joy interrupted, "I'll stop you right there. I don't need to be fixed up. Besides, I think I might have..." she stopped herself. She was going to tell her about the handsome doctor or the fact she was married, but she knew it would sound insane. She knew she'd sound like a lunatic if she didn't explain things right. Besides she was beginning to think she was losing her mind.

"You might have what?" Julie prodded.

"Never mind. I'm just happy by myself right now and fix ups never work out. You know that. Just because Eric is nice doesn't mean his friend will be nice and you really don't know Eric that well yet. Besides, what if things don't work out with Eric or worse. What if Eric turns out to be a serial killer? Then I'm stuck dating the best friend of a serial killer who incidentally may have killed my best friend," Joy joked.

"REALLY?! Really, Joy?!" exclaimed Julie as she flipped her red hair back with a bit of agitation.

"You need to control your temper. You know I'm kidding," Joy smiled and they both started laughing.

"Joy, you have a strange sense of humor," giggled Julie.

"KNOCK KNOCK, It's me, Nicole!" Nicole said from outside the door. Joy greeted Nicole at the door. Nicole was a serious smart brunette that was always overly cautious and had to plan everything. She considered herself a realist but Julie called her a pessimist.

31

She was the complete opposite of Julie. Julie was fun loving and adventurous, "I'll try anything once" type of person. Joy was so happy to have her best friends over so she could try to get a grip on what was going on.

After a little light chatting and catching up, Joy, Julie and Nicole sat down at the table to eat and have a serious discussion. The mood shifted in Joy's eyes and she became silent. Her friends took notice and leaned in to listen.

"Alright, enough small talk. What's this all about, are you okay?" asked Nicole.

"I'm not sure. It all started yesterday. I thought I was daydreaming but it was all so real," she told them. She went on and told them everything that happened. She told them how it happened and when it happened, as best she could remember. She told them about the bus and then she told them about David, Patricia, the doctor, and her husband.

"If this is all just my imagination, I can't explain the cut on my finger, the bandage being there," said Joy with concern.

Nicole looked solemn, "Are you completely certain you didn't cut your finger and bandage it yourself? Maybe you just don't remember doing it? Have you been

under a lot of stress? Stress can make you forget things."
She tried to comfort Joy.

"Yes, I'm positive," she nodded.

"Well, I think you just have a fantastic imagination! I think it sounds like a great place and I wouldn't worry. That doctor sounds like a hunk! If it happens again I would just explore and have fun with it. You haven't met your husband yet?" said Julie grinning ear to ear.

"Julie, I think Joy might need to see a psychiatrist or at least a doctor here. I don't think you should encourage her to entertain this fantasy world. She might have a personality disorder or a serious medical condition. I'm really concerned she might hurt herself," said Nicole.

Joy looked at Julie and said, "You always were a free spirit. I wish I didn't worry so much. I even thought it might be a brain tumor."

"My point exactly!" said Nicole with a stern face.

"Okay, well if it's her daydream or imagination then Joy should be able to control what is happening since it's her world," suggested Julie.

"Right, and?" Nicole prodded to find out where Julie was going with this idea.

"If it's really her daydream then she should try thinking good thoughts of what she wants to happen and see if it happens," Julie added.

"That's a good idea," said Joy.

"I think you should definitely keep us posted on what is going on and if we can help in any way just let us know," said Julie.

"Yes, I agree and don't worry, we won't tell anyone," said Nicole.

"We need to find out if you can control when this happens or if it's happening in one place like a worm hole," said Julie.

"I still think it's medical. But it wouldn't hurt for you to pay attention to when it happens and if you have control over it. So far it's only happening at work and you get dizzy spells. I'm no doctor, but I really think it's stress induced," Nicole added.

"You know there are all kinds of things in this world that can't be explained. We only use ten percent of our brains.." Julie said.

"Julie, that's a myth. We use our entire brain. The television and movies just perpetuate that old myth," Nicole interrupted.

"Oh, listen to Miss Know-it-all, so close-minded," Julie retaliated.

"Let's not argue, I was just stating a truth. We're here for Joy," Nicole reminded Julie.

"I was worried about not being able to come back. I worried about my pets. I don't know what I'd do if I couldn't get back here," said Joy nervously.

"I'll tell ya what," said Julie. "Get me a spare key to your house. I will text you or call you at least once a day to check on you. If you don't get back to me within a reasonable amount of time, then I will come over here and take care of your pets. I will also come looking for you. So, from now on if you feel stuck when you get there, just relax. You can text me from there too and let me know what is going on."

"I'll check in with you at least once a day too, but promise me you'll go see a doctor before this thing gets out of control," said Nicole.

"Okay, I promise." Joy smiled she felt better already. She knew her friends were there for her. She felt loved and secure at this moment. Joy, Julie and Nicole began talking about the past. They laughed about silly memories and cracked jokes the rest of the evening.

Chapter Four

Joy suddenly found herself walking down a long dirt road. She didn't know how she got here but she really didn't care. She wasn't sure if she was on Goose Island again.   It didn't seem like the island but she hadn't really seen much of the island yet. The dirt road was lined with lush forest trees. She walked for a long time. She approached a farm and there was a sign out front it said COW FOR SALE. She walked up to the farm house and knocked on the door. The farmer came to the door.

"I'd like to buy your cow. How much do you want?" Joy asked.

"Six hundred dollars," he answered.

She thought that sounded like a good price. Joy handed the farmer the money and she took the cow home. She named her Bessie and put her in her backyard. She began to wonder why she bought the cow. After all, she had a small back yard and lived in the city. She was pretty sure the city wouldn't let her keep the cow.

She was looking forward to getting milk from the cow, but she began to worry. She knew the cow would tear up her lawn. She also never had a cow before so she wasn't sure what to feed it or how much. She was certain the neighbor that lived behind her would turn her in for owning a cow in the city.

She didn't get along well with that neighbor. He liked to argue with her about everything from property lines to trees.

Just then, her alarm went off and she woke up.

"Oh," she sighed, "Thank God that was only a dream." She looked at Fitch and said, "It's not bad enough I have to figure out when I'm in the real world or on Goose Island but I also have to deal with my crazy dreams too, ugh!"

Joy got dressed and headed off to work. She looked at her work computer and logged in, it was 7:55 am. She was actually feeling a bit excited and looking forward to going back to Goose Island now.   She was only worried it might not happen now that she was so excited to go.

She made sure her cell phone was in her pocket so she could keep her friends informed. She started thinking good thoughts about what the entire Island looked like and what Michael would be like and how he would look. She thought of her dream man with wavy brown hair and beautiful hazel eyes. She pictured his smile and thought how kind he would be. She knew he would have a great sense of humor and make her laugh.

The next moment she was back in David and Patricia's home. The time schedule never made sense to her. It was now morning the day after she had cut her finger and she was sitting on their couch mid conversation with David. She didn't know what they had been talking about but David was talking to her like everything was normal.

She thought to herself, "okay try to control the outcome and the environment. I need to think of what I want to experience here."

"So, I know Patricia wants you to see Dr. Lewis today, but I agree with you. I think I should take you around the island and let you get familiar with your surroundings. I bet once you start seeing things like the town, your friends, your home, your dog..." said David

"Wait, my dog? I have a dog?" asked Joy.

"Yes, your dog Honey, she is a Golden Retriever and she's about two years old. She's such a good dog. Patricia and I have been feeding her while Michael is away and since you've been here with us. In fact, Patricia is out running errands right now and she'll be stopping over there about nine or so to feed Honey and let her out," he answered.

"Where did Michael go?" Joy asked.

"Oh he went to the mainland on business. He should be back soon," David told her.

"When can we go for a drive?" she asked.

"Anytime you are ready," David smiled.

"Okay, I'm ready now!" Joy said gleefully.

David and Joy walked out to the car. David held the car door open for Joy. He drove a 1980 yellow Cadillac Eldorado Biarritz. It was a Regal Coach Edition with a stainless steel top. It looked like a very expensive car and Joy hadn't seen a car quite like this one before.

"This is a gorgeous car, David." Joy told him as she slid onto the leather seat.

"Yes, it's my baby. I don't let Patricia drive it. If I had my say she wouldn't even ride in it, hahaha," he laughed. "Make yourself comfortable."

David started the engine and it purred. They pulled out of the driveway and onto the winding wooded road. The ride was smooth and Joy enjoyed the view. As they got closer to the edge of the island she could see the water peeking through the trees. The light reflecting on the water shimmered and rays of light danced all over the landscape between the trees and foliage.

"Does anything look familiar yet," David asked her.

Joy shook her head, "Nothing."

"I have an idea. Let's go to the art gallery on Main Street first. You spend a lot of time there," David suggested.

"I do? Why? Do I work there?" she asked curiously.

"Sort of, you own the place. Well, really you own this whole island," he told her.

Joy was shocked her good thoughts must be working. She was getting more excited with every second that passed. The scenery began to change a bit as they approached the town. The houses got a little smaller and closer together. Soon they were turning off the Outer Drive onto Main Street.

There was a gas station on the corner of Outer Drive and Main Street. Then a little further down a

40

grocery store. Joy soaked in all of the images. She saw the name of one of the stores was SWEATERS FOR SNAKES.

"That's odd," she said.

"What, dear?" asked David

"That store is called "Sweaters For Snakes". I find that a little strange," she told him.

"You do? Well, that's Angie's store. Your friend Angie, remember?" David told her. Joy looked puzzled.

"Angie, she's that little red headed friend of yours. You two have been friends forever." David turned the car around and went back to the store.

Joy became very curious and wondered if Angie looked like Julie. In her real life Julie had been her friend forever and she had red hair. She was trying to stay in the moment and enjoy her experience. She was worried if she thought too much about Julie that she might end up back at her desk. She focused her thoughts on the island.

David pulled up to the store and parked right in front. He walked around and opened the door for Joy. She got out of the car, and they walked into the store.

"Joy! Are you feeling better?" Angie asked with excitement. She didn't look anything like Julie. Angie was a cute little cheerleader type. She wasn't really the kind of person that Joy was friends with in the real world, but there was something about her that made Joy feel comfortable. Maybe it was her red hair or maybe it was just knowing she had a friend there.

David pulled Angie aside while Joy looked around the store on her way in. David told Angie quietly, "She's still not quite herself. She's lost her memory and I'm trying to help her remember."

"Oh, I see," Angie whispered back.

Joy walked towards Angie, "so, sweaters for snakes, huh? Is this a pet store because I don't really see much here but a lot of knitted..."

Angie snapped at her, "It's NOT a pet store! It's a clothing store for snakes."

"Uh....Just snakes?" Joy asked.

"Yes, *just* snakes," she answered sharply.

Joy looked really confused, "Soooo, you make a lot of money selling snake sweaters on the island?"

"I do very well thank you," Angie said happily.

"Oh, you probably sell worldwide on the web, right?" asked Joy.

"The what? Web? Ewwww, no. I hate spiders!" Angie scrunched her nose.

"No, you know, the internet." Joy explained. David and Angie looked at each other and then at Joy. David asked, "Do you feel alright, Joy? You are talking gibberish now."

"Yes, of course I'm fine. You mean you've never heard of the internet?"

She began thinking saying that was a mistake. She didn't want David and Angie to think she was crazy.

"No" they answered together.

"Oh never mind, I think I read an article about this new thing in a science magazine," she said quickly and dropped the subject.

"Anyhow, YOU! Angie! Selling snake sweaters, how cool," she smiled.

"Yeah, and I made them all myself," Angie said proudly.

"Well they are very beautiful," Joy told her.

"Maybe we should get on down to the art gallery now, whaddya think?" David asked.

"Oh yeah, sounds like a great idea," Joy answered.

As David walked ahead of her to open the door she reached in her pocket to grab her cell phone. While David wasn't looking she pulled her cell phone out quickly to see if she could send a message, but there was no signal. She shoved it back into her pocket quickly, but Angie saw what she did. Angie didn't say anything but she was curious.

"We can walk to the gallery from here if you're up to it," David said.

"That sounds like a good idea. I could use some fresh air and a little exercise," Joy told him.

"Exercise, what's that?" David asked.

Joy looked at David really concerned and wondered if the people of this island had never heard of exercise.   After the conversation about the internet she wasn't sure what was okay to talk about.

"Hahahaha, don't look so worried. I'm just joking," David laughed and Joy laughed with him.

As they walked from the sweater store to the gallery David made small talk with Joy. Only he forgot what Patricia had told him NOT to say.

"With Michael being away he won't even know you were missing," David let it slip.

"What do you mean missing?" asked Joy.

"Oh...well..uh..." David stuttered, "..uh yeah, you were missing and Patricia and I found you at the beach."

It sort of made sense to Joy, but she wondered why she was missing. Joy felt like David was hiding something from her. She was tempted to ask him why she was missing. She could see that she had already made David uncomfortable. So she didn't persist in questioning him, because she thought David was nice and she liked him.

David rapidly changed the subject and began talking about his car again, as they walked toward the art gallery.

Chapter Five

David and Joy arrived at the Goose Island art gallery. She looked up
and the sign said ART GALLERY OF JOY. David opened the door
and welcomed her into the gallery. Joy couldn't believe her eyes.
She looked around the room and every wall was filled with her
doodles framed and hung like art.

She looked at David with a puzzled face, "I don't understand.
These are my doodles...people buy them?"

"Buy them?! Yes they buy them," David exclaimed, "You've
sold enough of these to buy and own this entire island. Michael
doesn't even have to work because you've made so much money. He
enjoys working, gives him purpose I suppose."

"But they are just doodles. I mean, look at this one it's just a
spiral," she walked over and pointed at the framed drawing. "..and
this one, it's just a scribble!" She recognized two of the doodles that
she drew at work in the real world just yesterday. She looked around

some more and there were sculptures of doodles on pedestals. On one pedestal was a triangle and on another pedestal a spiral.

"Joy, your artwork is wonderful. Why Patricia and I bought three of your pieces. You didn't notice the picture hanging over the couch in the living room, did you?" David asked.

Just then the bells on the gallery door jingled as a middle aged man stuck his head inside, "Are you open, Joy?" asked the man.

Joy hesitated to say anything as she examined the man. The man had jet black hair with a few grays poking through. He had a five o'clock shadow but it was still before noon. He had a large prominent nose and a chummy smile. He was wearing a blue flowered Hawaiian shirt with ripped jeans and expensive tennis shoes.

"Come in," she said.

"Joy isn't quite herself today, Fred. She's having some trouble with her memory," David told him.

"Oh, what happened?" Fred asked.

"Well, we think she hit her head when she was down at the docks at Thunder Bay," David explained.

"Has she seen the doctor?" Fred asked.

"Where are my manners?" David changed the subject, "Joy, this is Fred he's our friendly pharmacist here in town. You'll find him to be very helpful and probably one of the nicest men you'll ever meet."

"Nice to meet you, Fred. But I guess we already know each other," Joy reached out to shake his hand.

"Oh, just give me a hug, Joy, you silly girl," Fred swooped in and hugged her. He picked her up off the ground and spun her around in a circle, then set her back down.

"Woo!" said Joy as her feet landed back on the floor.

"Oh, I'm sorry did I make you dizzy?" asked Fred.

"I'm okay." Joy answered.

"I saw the police at your pharmacy the other day. What happened?" David asked.

"Someone threw some rocks through the window of the pharmacy and broke in," Fred answered.

"That's just awful. What's this world coming to? Did they take anything?" David asked.

"Yes, they emptied the cash register and took several drugs. I'm really not supposed to talk about it while they investigate," Fred explained. "Hey Joy, what were you doing down at Thunder Bay?"

"Did you need something?" Joy asked nervously to avoid his question.

"Yes! I just came in to buy another one of your pieces of art. I have a blank wall in my dining room and I wanted to find something that would match the other piece I bought here last week," Fred said with enthusiasm.

Joy took over and it became natural for her to show him around. She showed him several of her doodles. They walked to the back of the gallery and Fred shouted, "It's perfect!"

He pointed at what appeared to be a blank canvas. As they got closer Joy could see just a drawing of an egg shape that was about a half inch high. It wasn't centered but offset down and to the left. She pulled it off the wall.

Fred said, "Let me help you, so you don't hurt yourself."

"Thank you, Fred." Joy smiled.

Fred noticed a sculpture as they walked toward the front of the gallery, "Joy, I really love that one," he pointed as he asked , "Will you set that one aside for me? I can pick it up next week."

"Sure!" Joy beamed. She was really getting into the feeling of being an artist and owning her own gallery.

They went to the cash register and Fred pulled the tag off the back and handed it to her so she could ring him up. Joy couldn't believe her eyes when she saw the price tag of $15,000. She gasped. She glanced at a few other price tags and saw one marked $50,000 and another for $65,000.

"Are you sure this is right?" she asked Fred.

"Oh dear, do you want more?" Fred seemed concerned.

"No..no," she stuttered. "Will this be cash, check or charge?"

Fred pulled out his checkbook and wrote Joy a check for the full amount. She was so excited to earn so much money for her little doodle. "I wish this were my real life," she thought to herself.

Fred said his goodbyes and took his new piece of art with him. Joy continued to look around the gallery, she was just astonished. David tapped her on the shoulder and startled her.

"You are beginning to look a little pale, dear. Maybe we should go grab a bite to eat." David suggested.

"I'm not really hungry," Joy answered.

"Patricia won't forgive me for taking you out and letting you skip your doctor visit if something happens to you," David said with concern.

"Well, maybe we could sit down somewhere and grab a cup of coffee?" she asked.

"I know just the place," David smiled.

David and Joy locked up the art gallery and walked across the street and over one block to a little Mom and

Pop restaurant simply called EAT HERE. Joy giggled a bit when she saw the name of the restaurant.

"What?" David asked.

"Oh, I just thought it was funny the restaurant is just called "Eat Here.""

"Mr. and Mrs. Little own the restaurant and they argued over what to name it. Jack - that's Mr. Little - wanted to name it something nautical and Marge, his wife, wanted to name it after her Mother Fanny. Jack thought "Fanny's" was not a good name for a restaurant since that's also a slang term for a body part. And I'll just say, you don't want to associate that part with food, unless you're talkn' about rump roast hahaha. Jack also didn't like his Mother in law very well.   Marge began doing little things to annoy Jack such as making his meals at home taste bad. She would also send him out in wrinkled shirts and pants because she was irritated that he wouldn't let her name the restaurant Fanny's. Jack is the one with the money but Marge runs the restaurant and the marriage. So, after months of bickering and not having a sign up, Jack finally just had the painter hang up this sign," David pointed at the sign.

David swung open the door and held it for Joy. She looked around at the booths and they grabbed one by the window. They both sat down and Marge came rushing over.

"Hey, David, Joy how are ya?" Marge asked. She was a portly woman with curly black hair and a large mole on her cheek near her nose. She had dark eyes but a friendly smile. She handed them a couple of menus.

"We're fine, just fine," David answered.

"Fine," Joy echoed.

"What can I get you to drink?"

"I'll just have a cup of black coffee for now," Joy answered.

"Okay, and you, David?"

"I'll have the same," David smiled. "Where's Jack today?"

"He went fishing early this morning with the boys. I suppose they are either still out there...drinking by now, it's such a nice sunny day. Or maybe they caught some fish and went home to nap," Marge told him. "He just better not be cleaning those fish in my kitchen."

David chuckled, "Well maybe he should set up a cleaning station out by his shed. That would keep the fish out of your kitchen."

"Yea, if I could get him to pay someone to make one. He's too lazy to build one himself and too cheap to pay anyone," said Marge. "Well, I'll get your coffee and you can have a look at the menu."

The sun was warming Joy's face as it shined in the window of the restaurant. She closed her eyes for a moment just enjoying the warmth of the sun on her skin.

"The sun is in your eyes, do you want me to close this blind?" David asked.

"NO, it feels good, the snow is six inches deep back..." Joy didn't finish her sentence.

David looked at her oddly, "Maybe I was wrong in bringing you out. Maybe you *should* go see Dr. Lewis."

"I'm sorry, really I'm okay. I was just thinking about something else. The sun feels good," Joy answered quickly.

"Here's your coffee," Marge poured the hot coffee into their cups. The steam rose up and fogged David's glasses as he took a sip. Marge took out her waitress tablet and pen and asked, "What would you like?"

"I'll have the triple decker bacon cheeseburger with a side salad. I gotta watch my figure you know," David joked.

"What kind of dressing do you want on your salad?"

"I'll have the house dressing," David replied.

53

"Do you want fries with your burger?" Marge asked.

"Sure, twist my arm why don't cha?" answered David in jest.

"And you?" Marge asked Joy.

"I guess I'll have some wheat toast with jam," answered Joy.

"That's all?" Marge asked.

"She's not hungry," David interjected.

"Okay darlin', I'll get that right out."

Marge hustled back to the kitchen to make their food. The smells coming from the kitchen were making Joy's appetite increase. She could hear the bacon sizzle and the aroma soon followed. The cooking utensils clanked on the grill as the food was prepared.

"David, since I don't remember anything could you tell me about Michael?"

"I don't know what to tell you. He's a great son and he's been a good husband to you. He makes you laugh. You once told me he makes you very happy. Everyone on the island loves you and Michael. You're just the perfect couple as far as everyone is concerned," David answered genuinely.

"I think I'd like to go home when we're done here," Joy told him.

"If that's what you want, I'll take you home. After all you aren't being held hostage or anything. Patricia might get upset, but she will get over it. I will tell her she can check in on you, if that's alright with you?"

Joy smiled, "Of course, that would be wonderful. I would like to see if anything at home jogs my memory."

Marge brought out the food, "Here's your salad, David and here's your toast, Hun. I'll be right back with your burger."

"Mmmm, this looks good!" David put his napkin in his lap.

The two of them ate quietly and just enjoyed the atmosphere. Then Marge came back and said, "Here's your burger and fries, enjoy!"

"Honey, will be happy to see you," David told Joy.

"Honey? Oh that's right, my dog," she remembered what he had told her earlier. "Yes, I bet she will."

Then Joy thought about her cat Fitch and her two goldfish and she missed them. But she remembered that Julie promised to look after them if something happened to her.

Chapter Six

David and Joy got into his Cadillac and he drove back
down Main Street towards Outer Drive. He pointed at the
hardware store, "That's my little shop."

"The hardware store?" she asked.

"Yes, I work there a couple days a week, but I own
the store," David's face lit up when he talked about his
store. "It's a good excuse to get away from the wife when
she's getting on my nerves."

David signaled to turn left and they turned onto
Outer Drive. They were headed away from Patricia and
David's house. Joy saw the beach and the docks where
they had pulled her out of the water. She could still see
some boats out in the bay. The water was fairly calm
today.

"That's Thunder Bay," David told her as he
continued driving. "Outer Drive goes all the way around

the island. You live high up on the ridge that overlooks the water."

They began to ascend as Outer Drive went upward into a very scenic area of the island. Joy was able to see small waves crashing onto the beach. They approached an area covered in trees again. This side of the island had large boulders near the road, some of the road was cut into the rock. Every now and then she'd get a glimpse of the water through the trees.

Joy began to wonder about her husband again. She knew David and Patricia were quite a bit older than her parents. It made her wonder how old Michael was. In real life, Joy's parents had both passed away tragically. They died in an automobile accident because the other driver was texting and hit them head on.

"David, how old is Michael?" Joy inquired.

"Let's see, Michael turns forty-six this year. His birthday isn't far off," David told her.

Joy was in her early thirties and had always dated men closer to her age. She knew that people in their forties appearance could vary quite spectacularly. She began to worry he might look old, fat and bald. She also knew people in their twenties that had aged significantly. One guy she went to school with in the real world had lost his hair by their five year reunion. On the other hand, she had seen older men that were quite attractive.

"Do we have -um- children?" she asked nervously.

"No, Joy."

David put his blinker on to make a right turn as he slowed down she saw her driveway. As he pulled up to the house, it was the house she had always imagined. In her real life, she always thought if she won the lottery she would buy a home exactly like this. It was a beautiful large home with harbor blue siding and white trim. There was a three car garage that was attached to the home. It was actually slightly more grand than what she had imagined. The yard was professionally landscaped and there was a gorgeous variety of trees, shrubs and flowers in all the right places. She looked around and saw magnolia trees and majestic pines.

David and Joy got out of the car and walked up to the house. "Here, I think I have your spare key," He said as he fumbled through his pockets. David pulled the key from his pocket and handed it to Joy.

"Thank you," Joy took the key and opened the door to her dream home. Honey came running and wagging her tail. She was so excited to see Joy. "Hi, Honey!" she ran her hands all over her dog. She got down on her knees and hugged Honey while Honey licked Joy's cheek.

"I think I'll let you get comfortable in your home and I better go home and tell Patricia I brought you back here. That is, if you feel alright," David told her.

"Yes, I'll be fine," Joy told him. She was looking forward to exploring her home. "I hope Patricia doesn't get upset with you."

"Aww, don't worry. After being married for so many years, I'm used to her getting upset. When she gets that way I just go to work. Hahahaha!" David laughed.

David gave her a hug and he left. She watched him drive away. She loved everything about this home and it's décor, it was all her. The living room had a cozy clean beach home feeling. There was a fireplace with a large white mantel. On the mantel was a photograph of her and five men. She wondered if one of them was her husband. Honey stayed right on Joy's heels as she walked around the house.

Joy walked through to the back of the home. The view was magnificent. She had large open windows and glass doors that opened to the beach. She walked out in the backyard and there were more lovely trees and flowers. In the backyard there were several large oak trees, a spruce, and some cherry trees. She looked to the right and there was a path that went down the hill to the beach.

"Honey, do you want to go for a walk?" Joy asked.

Honey barked and wagged her tail. They began to walk down the path toward the beach. The path was lined with exotic flowers. She recognized many of them but some she had never seen before. She wondered if they existed in the real world or just this one.

She could hear the waves gently crashing on the beach. She stopped and smelled some of the unusual flowers along the path. She got to the bottom of the path and took her shoes off so she could walk in the sand. Off to the left there was a rack for kayaks and canoes. There was one canoe with it's paddles and room for two kayaks. It appeared one kayak was missing. She didn't think too much about it.

She walked closer to the water and Honey tagged along. It was a beautiful day and perfect for a walk along the beach. She found a couple of flat rocks and stepped into the edge of the water, it was cold. She skipped the rocks across the water and continued to walk along the beach in the sand.

It was quite a while before she saw another home but it was magnificent as well. Each home she saw along this beach area looked like one mansion after another. After a while, she decided she better turn back and go home. She knew the sun would be going down soon but that she still had time to get back home before it got dark.

Joy called Honey to come along as she turned back toward the house. Honey brought her a stick.

"Oh, you want to play?" Joy asked Honey.

Joy tugged on the stick and Honey tugged back playfully. Honey finally let loose and Joy threw the stick. Honey chased after it and brought it back. They did this a few times and then Honey saw a cat in the window of one of the homes. Honey started barking at the cat.

"What do you see?" Joy looked and saw the black cat sitting inside on the ledge of the window. "Oh calm down. It's just a cat. Am I going to have to put you on a leash?"

She managed to get Honey to listen and they completed their walk home. She saw the canoe and kayak again. Then she found her path back to the house. They walked up the path and the sun was starting to get low. She thought it would be nice to watch the sun set from her backyard. The air was getting a bit chilly. She went inside and found a blanket and curled up on the patio lounge chair. Honey jumped up by her feet.

After the sun went down she took Honey inside and began looking around the house again. She walked into the kitchen and loved her white planked cabinets. The green granite counter top was elegant. Joy played with the lighting.

Honey walked over with her dish in her mouth. Joy looked down at her. "Oh, you must be hungry?" Joy looked through closet doors in the kitchen until she found where the dog food was stashed away. She found a scoop in the bag and put a scoop of dog food in her dish.

Honey picked up one piece of food from her dish. She walked over to an area rug and plopped down to eat the one piece of dog food. Then she got up and repeated this action over and over.

She heard a phone ring. It was a wall phone. She answered, "Hello?"

"Hello, Joy?" Patricia answered.

"Oh, is this Patricia?" Joy asked.

"Yes, are you doing okay?"

"Yes, I took Honey for a walk on the beach and we sat out on the patio and watched the sun go down. Now I'm just getting familiar with my place," Joy told her.

"David told me you didn't go see Dr. Lewis today."

"Yes, he thought you'd be upset," Joy answered.

"No, maybe it's better that you went out and did what you did. Maybe it will help you remember," Patricia said. "Listen, my phone number is on the list of numbers on the wall next to your phone. Do you see it?"

Joy looked at the list, "Yes, yes I see it."

"If you need me, call me and I'll be right over. I talked to Michael today and he's coming home earlier than expected. He's worried about you too," Patricia told her.

Joy got a little anxious, "Did he say when he will be home?"

"No, but he's going to try to get here tomorrow night," Patricia replied.

"Okay, well I'm going to take a bath and get to bed," Joy said.

"Alright, goodnight." Patricia said.

"Goodnight." said Joy.

Joy hung up the phone and remembered her cell phone in her pocket. She pulled it out again and tried to get a signal but nothing happened. In fact, now her phone had nearly lost it's entire charge.

Joy noticed the answering machine next to the phone had a message blinking. She played the message back.

The machine went "beep you have one message....Hi Joy, this is Beth your life and fitness coach! I was just checking in to see why you missed your last two appointments with me. I hope everything's okay. Call me!"

She looked at Honey. Honey was dirty from the walk on the beach. She had gotten quite muddy running along the waters edge chasing sticks.

"You look like you could use a bath too." Joy led Honey into the bathroom and got the tub ready to bathe the dog. Honey didn't want a bath. Joy shut the bathroom door to keep Honey from running out of the room. She struggled to get Honey into the tub. Honey was a heavy dog. Joy would lift her front legs in and just as she would push Honey's back legs in, Honey would get her front legs out of the tub.

Finally after several attempts, Joy got the entire dog into the tub. She began to pour warm water on her and soap her up. After she got her all foamy with suds she rinsed her off.

Honey shook water all over Joy and the bathroom, "Ahhh!" Joy yelled. She grabbed a large towel out of the cupboard and began drying Honey.

"I think I need to find the hair dryer for you," Joy told Honey.

Joy searched through drawers and cupboards until she found the dryer and a brush. She put the dryer on low and brushed Honey as she dried her. Once she finished she cleaned up the bathroom. She felt like she had quite the work out.

"My turn," Joy said in an exhausted voice as she cleaned the tub.

She ran her bath and enjoyed a nice long soak. When she was done, she found a robe hanging behind the door and wrapped her hair in a towel. She walked upstairs and found her master bedroom which incidentally had a much bigger bath attached. She went into her master bathroom and took the towel off her head. She noticed she had the most expensive lotions and creams. She tried a few of the expensive facial creams. She dried her hair and walked into the bedroom.

Joy walked over to the walk in closet and found some pajamas. She saw Micheal's clothes hanging on one side of the closet and her clothes on the other side. They both had a lot of shoes.

She opened her jewelry chest and found it packed with treasure. She had a very large stand up jewelry chest. She opened the top and it was full of rings. She never wore a lot of jewelry and certainly couldn't imagine wearing all of this. She opened the two doors to reveal beautiful diamond, ruby, and emerald necklaces dangling in front of her eyes. There were more drawers but she was too tired to keep looking.

Joy put on her pajamas and crawled into the fluffy soft bed. She snuggled in for a good night of sleep.

Honey jumped up on the bed and curled up by Joy's feet. Joy dozed off.

Joy woke up back at her desk in the real world. The computer clock read 11:06am and it was the same day in the real world. She felt drained of energy. She was worried and thought to herself, "It's been three hours since I logged in. I wonder if anyone noticed anything." She was afraid to ask, she was sure they would tell her if she was sleeping or something.

Her computer was still on and it looked like she had been working but not real fast. She pulled her cell phone out of her pocket and it was dead, so she plugged it in to charge. The phone at her desk rang and she answered. It was a customer and she began working. She yawned and just wanted to crawl back into that soft cozy bed. At lunch time she sent a text message to Julie and Nicole.

Text, "I was just there again. I lost three hours here but I was on Goose Island for an entire day. It was amazing and wonderful. I will call you tonight."

Julie messaged her back, "How awesome! I can't wait to hear all about it!"

Nicole messaged her back, "Okay talk to you soon. Did you call the doctor?"

Joy ignored Nicole's question, she wasn't quite ready to tell a doctor about what was going on.

Now, she was a little worried about Honey. She wondered if Honey would be okay, but she recalled how she had been mid conversation with David when she arrived that morning. She tried to reassure herself that everything would be fine.

Joy felt like she needed to go to bed but she still had more than a half day of work ahead of her. After that, the long drive home. She knew the day would be brutal. She would just have to power through.

Chapter Seven

Joy arrived home that evening and Fitch greeted her at the door. She set her purse on the kitchen counter and left her shoes by the door. Then she picked up her cat in her arms to give her a hug but Fitch hissed and ran to hide under a small end table. "Huh?" she thought to herself, "I wonder if Fitch can smell Honey on me? She's never acted like that."

Joy got the cat food and filled her dish. She called her, "here kitty kitty kitty."

Fitch peeked out and walked over cautiously. When she felt safe she began eating her dinner. Joy stroked her cat's head gently to assure her that everything was fine. Fitch began to purr.

Joy took off her winter coat and hung it up in the closet. Then she walked over and fed her goldfish. She was pretty hungry herself, but she was also very tired. She didn't know if she just wanted to flop down on her couch and fall asleep or eat something. She also knew she promised to call her friends.

Joy walked over to her refrigerator and opened the door. She saw a jar of pickles, expired milk, a head of lettuce, an old zucchini, one onion, two boiled eggs, and a couple of wine coolers.

"Ugh, I guess it's frozen dinner night," she thought as she closed the refrigerator door and reached into her freezer. It was pretty empty up there too.

"I'll have to find some time to go shopping," she thought.

With her eight hour work day, an hour for lunch and about an hour total commute it really cut into her weekdays. She barely had time for errands let alone a social life. She was usually fatigued when she got home anyhow, but today was worse.

She put the frozen dinner in the microwave and picked up her cell phone to call Julie.

"Hello?" Julie answered.

"Hi, so it happened again. I spent an entire day with my father in-law exploring the island and talking. I ended up back at my gorgeous home on the beach," Joy explained.

"Wow! I need to hear all the details," Julie said eagerly.

"Well, what was really strange is this time I didn't wake up in bed. I was just sitting on the couch in his living room. Apparently we were having a conversation and he didn't seem to notice anything odd," Joy told her.

"Didn't you say the first time you just washed up on shore?" Julie asked.

"Yes, the second time I woke up in bed," Joy told her.

"And when you go there does it ever happen anywhere other than work?" Julie prodded.

"Not yet, it's always happened when I've been sitting at my desk. I think I do control things because I own the island and it's like a dream come true. It's all just too perfect. But some things I just really question because it's not stuff I would think of," Joy answered.

"Like what?" Julie asked.

"For instance, there is a store on the island that just sells sweaters for snakes. It's such an oddball thing, don't you think? And I certainly never could have dreamed that up by myself," Joy told her.

"Hmmm, that is strange," Julie said.

"I'm also having a really hard time keeping track of what time or day it is. I'm basically living through two days or a day and half day in one day. It's so confusing and this last day just took it's toll on me," Joy told her.

"Tell me more about the island, did you meet Michael?" Julie was thrilled to learn more.

"I am really tired and I need to eat dinner and I still haven't talked to Nicole. Can we talk about it later or maybe this weekend?" Joy asked.

"I can call Nicole and let her know, that way you can get some rest," said Julie.

"Okay, thanks I really appreciate that," Joy said with a sigh.

"Okay I'll talk to you later, bye," Julie said.

"Bye," said Joy as she hung up.

Her microwave had beeped while she was talking to Julie. Joy opened the microwave and peeled the film of plastic off her dinner. She sat down at the table and ate. She couldn't think she was so tired. She went straight to bed.

Julie kept her promise and called Nicole just as soon as she got off the phone with her friend Joy, "Hello, Nicole?"

"Hi Julie, what's up?" Nicole asked.

"I just got off the phone with Joy. She said she was supposed to call you, but she's really tired and had to eat dinner," said Julie.

"I'm really worried about her. I think she's avoiding calling me because she is avoiding seeing a doctor. She really needs to go talk to a medical professional. She could be in trouble. I know you think this is all fun and games, but Joy's life should not be your entertainment," Nicole said sharply.

"I'm worried about her too!" Julie whined, "I can't help it if I find it all so interesting."

"If you really care about her, then do something about it. You need to back me up on this. The next time you talk to her just suggest that it would be a good idea to go see the doctor. Tell her that you or I will go with her if she likes," Nicole said in a serious tone. "Joy has been complaining of headaches and dizzy spells, that really bothers me. She also talks about being tired, she's been withdrawn. You know she could be suffering from depression or multiple problems."

"Okay, I will. I'm not sure that I agree with you but if we could rule out the medical scenario then maybe we can really find out what's going on," Julie said.

"Oh, like worm holes?" Nicole said sarcastically.

"Yea, maybe!" Julie said defensively.

"Maybe it wouldn't hurt for you to see that doctor too," Nicole nipped back at her.

"Nicole, you are just so pessimistic about everything. You think everyone is out to hurt you or rip you off. Honestly, I don't know how you have ANY fun!" Julie blurted back.

"I'm sorry, I didn't mean to hurt your feelings. You know I don't always mean what I say. I guess I'm just really so upset that we could lose our friend and we don't know what is happening to her. I just want what's best for her. You know she's all alone with no family. We're her only family," Nicole apologized.

"I know. When she lost her parents it was so devastating. She withdrew from everyone and everything," Julie added.

"And that job is really isolating her too," said Nicole.

"I really do want to know she is safe. Most of all, I want Joy to be happy. She hasn't been happy in a long time. She seems to be enjoying whatever this thing is and it's great to see her smile again," Julie said.

"Then let's help her," Nicole told her.

"Okay, we'll work together to figure this thing out. Good or bad we'll get her through this," said Julie.

"I'll text you the name and phone number of a good doctor she can talk to and you can pass that along to her, because I don't think she's listening to me," said Nicole.

"That's fine, I will give it to her the next time I meet with her," said Julie agreeably.

"Alright, stay in touch, let me know how she reacts, and keep me posted, bye," said Nicole.

"Okay, bye," Julie repeated.

Fitch woke Joy up again just as she always did. Joy felt the cat pulling her hair and then her rough tongue licking her face. Fitch began kneading Joy's belly with her paws.

"Fitch, the alarm hasn't even gone off yet. Let me sleep, please!" Joy begged.

About ten minutes later her alarm clock began buzzing. Joy rolled over with her messy blonde hair in her face and she groaned. She knew she had to get up. She rolled off the bed and went THUNK! on the floor.

"Owwwww!" Joy got up slowly. The alarm was still buzzing so she turned it off. She walked into the bathroom and looked at her face. She had fallen asleep in her clothes from the previous day and her makeup was smeared all over her face. Black mascara and eyeliner covered her eyes. It was not as it was meant to be but, more like she had two black eyes. She turned on the faucet and began putting cold water on her face. She grabbed her make up remover and began wiping the dark circles away.

Joy weighed herself each day. She wasn't super fit but she had a nice figure. She stopped going to the gym when her parents died. Today she got on the scale and was dismayed to see she had gained five pounds. She decided it must be that she was eating five or six meals a day and she would need to be more careful. She knew if a cut could make it's way back from her daydream then it was possible she was making herself gain weight too. She still wasn't sure that she brought the injury from the daydream to the real world. She wasn't taking any chances.

She made up her mind she would try harder to control her fantasy of Goose Island, after all it seemed to work for her yesterday. She felt like things had gone pretty well and she was looking forward to trying it again today.

She also thought it would be a good idea to start keeping a journal of her visits so she could keep her thoughts straight. She didn't have time right now, she had to get ready for work. She decided she would start her journal tonight or if she found time on her lunch break.

Joy went in her kitchen and made a cup of coffee. She sat down and drank her coffee and rubbed her temples. Her temples felt tender and swollen.

"I think I'll need a lot of coffee today," she told Fitch as the cat rubbed up against her legs.

Joy finished her coffee and went to her bathroom to take a shower. She felt a dizzy spell while she was in the shower and thought this might be a good time to get out of the shower. She didn't want to fall and injure herself.

She thought about the dizzy spells she had been having and how normally they seemed to propel her into Goose Island or back into the real world. She waited a few minutes to see if anything was going to happen. When nothing happened she decided she had better hurry up and finish getting ready for work.

Joy arrived at work safely. She logged into her computer and began working. She did everything the same as usual but nothing was happening. She went through her entire normal routine, coffee, pacing, and thinking about Goose Island. It was nearly lunch time and she was still at work. She was getting a little sad.

When she went to lunch she felt a little sick so she didn't eat anything. She decided she probably didn't need it anyhow. She was feeling sleepy when she went back to her desk.

Paul came over to Joy's cubicle, "Hey, you know we are having a meeting today, right?" he asked.

She was startled since she wasn't used to people coming over to talk to her. She jumped a bit, "Oh, what?!" Joy asked.

"We have an office meeting today. The supervisor asked me to come around and remind everyone," Paul answered.

"Yes, I remember. I saw it in the memo the other day. But thanks for reminding me," she told him.

She slumped back down in her chair and began typing. She was actually starting to feel a little depressed that she couldn't escape the office today. She thought she was doing everything right to make it happen. "It's just my daydream, why isn't it happening like before?" she thought.

At two o'clock the entire office staff went into the meeting room. Joy was the last one to walk in. Everyone filed in and sat down at the meeting table. The boss made important announcements about changes and policies. He opened the floor for discussion. Each time Joy would try to ask a question someone would jump in and talk right over her. She felt invisible again.

The one time Joy didn't feel invisible at work was when she had just come out of the ladies room. One of her male co-workers was just about to go into the mens room. He stopped and said, "well hello," as he sort of laughed and was grinning ear to ear. Joy walked through an entire room of cubicles with people standing around talking.

When she rounded the corner into the room where she worked a female co-worker stopped her. The woman informed Joy that she had the back of her dress tucked into her underwear. Joy turned beet red and suddenly knew why everyone was looking at her.

Joy sat in the meeting barely listening to her other co-workers minor complaints about parking and other such issues. She sank down in her chair as she continued to feel unimportant and obscure.

And then it happened….she woke up in her bed at her home on Goose Island. There was a handsome man sitting on the edge of the bed and he had his hand on her head stroking her hair. The man had a kind friendly smile with dimples, golden brown wavy hair, and the most beautiful hazel eyes.

Joy thought she should be afraid because she didn't know who this man was, but deep down she felt that she did know him.

"How are you feeling, Joy?" he asked.

"Michael?" she asked.

__Chapter Eight__

Michael leaned in toward Joy and wrapped his arms around her. He hugged her softly and whispered, "Oh my love, you remember me."

Joy leaned back to look him in the eyes and told him, "Things are still a little fuzzy for me, but I'm getting better." She lied to him because she didn't want to hurt his feelings.

"How long was I sleeping? The last I knew you weren't coming home for a few days or you were trying to get home early? I can't remember," Joy added.

"Dad said he dropped you off here yesterday and Mom spoke to you on the phone last night," Michael answered.

The sun was shining in through the bedroom window as it began to rise. Joy figured out it was just the next morning. She felt well rested here, not like the real world. Back in the real world she was exhausted. She felt energized and renewed this morning.

"Do you have plans for today?" Michael asked.

"No, I just thought maybe I should try to remember more about you, about us," she told him timidly.

"Hmmm, that sounds like fun. It's a little like starting over. Meanwhile if you want to get dressed and come downstairs, I have made you breakfast," Michael smiled.

She couldn't take her eyes off his smile and his dimples. She was captivated at how handsome her husband looked. She thought how nice he seemed too. She watched him leave the room as he blew her a kiss.

A little while later Joy came down the stairs dressed in clothes that she wouldn't wear casually in her real life because they were too nice. It was the most casual clothing she could find in her closet and dresser. She felt fresh and affluent as she walked into her dining room.

"Oh, do you want to sit in the dining room or would you like to eat breakfast on the patio like you normally do? "Michael asked. "It's beautiful outside this morning."

Joy looked surprised, "I'll eat on the patio. That sounds great!"

"Good, It's all set up out there and I made your favorite," Michael told her.

Joy wondered if her favorite breakfast here would be the same as it was in the real world. It didn't matter, she knew it would be good.

Michael led her out onto the patio overlooking the ocean. The sun was shining and it was a perfect temperature outside. It wasn't too breezy and there was not a bug in sight. Michael pulled her chair away from the table so she could sit down. Joy sat down and Michael gave her a kiss on the cheek and placed a cloth napkin in her lap.

The food smelled delicious as she gazed upon the dishes. She looked around the table and saw a dish of fresh cut fruit, a stack of french toast, a pitcher of orange juice, and all of the necessary condiments. Michael filled her coffee cup with the best coffee she had ever smelled. He removed the lid from her plate to reveal her spinach, mushroom, and cheese omelet with bacon on the side. It was her favorite!

Everything in this daydream life was so much better than her real life. Her morning breakfast was perfect, her husband was heavenly, and her home was divine. Joy watched the waves of the ocean and enjoyed their rhythm. She became caught up in the view and her handsome company.

"I thought it would be a good idea to take you to our favorite place today and maybe another special spot," Michael told her.

Joy nodded eagerly as she fed herself another bite of her omelet. She sipped her coffee and asked, "Can you remind me how we met?"

Michael grinned, "Are you kidding me? You really must be joking. I can't believe you forgot how we met."

Joy shrugged, "I really did forget, I'm sorry."

"It's not your fault," he told her. "You bumped your head pretty hard."

"You didn't answer my question. Remind me how we met," she prodded.

"It was at one of your art shows. You were having a monumental unveiling of your latest works..." he started.

"How long had I been selling my artwork?" she interrupted.

"Well, you told me you had been doing artwork your entire life but it had just taken off in the five years prior to our meeting," he answered.

"And how long have we been married?" she asked.

"We've been married five wonderful years now," he smiled. "Anyhow, as I was telling you, I walked into your art show in New York City to look at your work. I had read good things about you."

Joy's mouth fell open, "My show in New York City?! Are you kidding me?!"

"No, I'm quite serious," Michael answered as he sipped some orange juice. "You are more talented than you realize. I can see you haven't forgotten your modesty."

Joy blushed, "It's just that...."she hesitated. "...well... I don't feel like I deserve all of this."

"Why shouldn't you deserve it? You are a hardworking, caring, talented lady. Why should one man be rich when another is poor? It's what you set your mind to be. That is what you become and that is what you deserve," Michael said with passion.

"Don't you think some of it is just chance or luck?" she questioned.

"Maybe a small part is left to fate. I think hard work and believing in what you do is the majority of your destiny and success," Michael told her as he held her hand softly and began caressing her gently.

"So, you were telling me how we met," Joy added.

"Your show was quite elegant. I walked in wearing my tuxedo. I wandered around admiring your unique artwork. You walked up to me and told me to get another plate of hors d'oeuvres. See, the waiters were also wearing black tuxedos. You thought I was one of the waiters," He told her.

"I didn't!" she was embarrassed.

"You did! I must say you were rude but very cute," Michael teased her.

"Rude?" she asked sheepishly.

"Yes, in fact after you told me to get another plate of hors d'oeuvres, you continued to lecture me about standing around doing nothing. You got quite upset and told me that you weren't paying me to stand around and do nothing. I could barely get a word in edgewise," he laughed.

"I don't believe you," Joy responded.

"You better believe me," he went on. "When you finally stopped talking and took a breath, I told you that I was not a waiter. You were rather embarrassed and you began apologizing. I told you that you could make it up to me by having dinner with me."

"And I fell for that line?" Joy asked.

"Well, I think you were attracted to me a little," he laughed. "And yes it seemed to work just fine. After your show we went to a fancy restaurant and we talked so much

I think neither one of us ate much of our food. After dinner we went for a nice walk in the city."

"It sounds wonderful," said Joy with a sigh.

Michael began clearing the dishes off the table and Honey came over to Joy with a ball. Before Michael could say "don't!", Joy took the ball and tossed it for Honey. Honey chased the ball into some bushes and came out with a few leaves stuck to her fur. She bounced across the yard wagging her tail and running toward Joy.

Michael tried calling Honey toward him but the dog wouldn't listen. Honey picked up speed, jumped and lunged toward Joy. Joy fell over backwards in her chair. Honey stood over Joy with her two front paws on Joy's chest. Honey wagged her tail and drooled.

"I tried to warn you, I guess you forgot how Honey plays fetch with balls," Michael apologized as he helped Joy dust off. He assisted in getting Joy up off the ground and he set her chair back up.

"Did she hurt you?" he asked.

"No," she said laughing, "I'm okay. She didn't act that way on the beach."

"You're lucky," Michael told her.

"I guess so," she replied. "I'll have to be more careful with her. She's about two years old your Dad told me, where did I get her?"

"You just brought her home as a puppy one day. You said you fell in love with her and had to have her. You told me you picked her up at a pet store when you were on the mainland," Michael answered.

Joy thought that didn't seem like something she would do. She would rather rescue a pet than buy one from a pet store. She knew a lot of puppies were bred in puppy mills and she didn't want to support that kind of activity. But she thought, "Maybe things are different here, I guess I'm different here."

"Are you ready to go see our favorite place?" Michael asked.

"Most definitely!" she said with excitement.

"Then come with me," Michael said as he extended his elbow so she could wrap her arm in his. She grabbed his arm to let him lead the way.

Chapter Nine

Michael opened the garage door to expose several vehicles. Joy's jaw dropped. There were several classic cars and that didn't even include the two new vehicles in the driveway. Michael walked over to the wall and grabbed a set of keys. Then he stepped over to his favorite car and opened the door.

"Well, don't just stand there silly, get in," he grinned.

Michael enjoyed driving his Chevrolet Corvette C3 Stingray and so it made sense this was the car he chose to drive today to take Joy to their favorite place. He revved the engine and pulled out of the garage.

It was another perfectly sunny day on Goose Island. The sunlight danced on the car as they drove down the wooded road. The ocean peeked through at Joy as she was lost in blissful thoughts. She felt like a child on

Christmas morning. She couldn't help but wonder what marvelous thing would happen next and where they were going.

Michael slammed on the brakes and jolted Joy out of her thoughts, "What?!" Joy screamed.

There was a little morning mist floating in the air and two majestic deer stood in the middle of the road directly in front of the car. There was a large buck standing beside his doe.

"Aren't they beautiful?" he asked Joy.

"Oh my goodness, wow! I've never seen deer so close before," she told him.

Michael looked at her curiously, "Yes you have."

Joy said, "Well, I just don't remember."

"It's a good thing I saw them. That bit of fog just came up suddenly. I should be used to it. I'm sorry I scared you," Michael told her.

They continued down from the ridge toward town. As they descended the view was amazing. They reached Main street and Michael put his blinker on to turn right. He slowed down as they passed the art gallery and he parked in front of Eat Here.

"Here we are!" Michael said happily.

Joy darted her head back and forth looking around wondering to herself, "Could it be something else? It surely couldn't be this simple little restaurant?"

Michael walked around and opened her car door, he obviously had gotten his manners from his Dad. Joy got out of the car and looked up at the sign, then she looked at Michael, "I was here with your Dad already."

"You were?" he acted surprised. "Well, I won't hold that against you," he said as he laughed.

He opened the door to the restaurant and as they walked in she told him, "I'm not hungry, we just ate."

"Neither am I," he told her as he grabbed her hand. He pulled her past several tables with people seated at them toward a booth in the corner. As they walked through the restaurant, many people greeted them by name. Joy didn't recognize any of them but answered hello in return. The smell of bacon, eggs, coffee, and pancakes filled the air.

"You see this booth?" Michael pointed. "This is where I first told you that I love you."

Joy smiled, "Ohhhhhh."

Marge walked out, "Back again I see, where do you want to sit?"

"Oh we aren't staying. I'm just taking Joy on a trip down memory lane," Michael told Marge.

"I see," Marge smiled. She headed back into the kitchen to finish her orders.

"Now we will go to our favorite spot," Michael told her as he grabbed her hand again to lead the way.

Everyone in the restaurant seemed to know who they were and liked them. All of the patrons told Michael and Joy "goodbye" or "see ya later, Joy!" or "You two have a nice day!"

Joy couldn't be more happy. She had a caring, loving man and a town full of people who loved her. Michael opened the car door to let Joy in and they were off again.

They drove to another part of the island that Joy hadn't seen yet. As the car slowed down Michael put on his turn signal and they turned down Golden Road. The road was lined with cherry trees and magnolia trees. The trees were in full bloom. Flower petals made a carpet of color on the road. A variety of birds fluttered around as they drove up the road. Joy saw a sign "WILDLIFE SANCTUARY NEXT RIGHT".

Michael put his blinker on again to turn right and pulled into the wildlife sanctuary. He pulled into the lot and parked the car.

"Is it coming back to you yet?" he asked.

"I'm sorry, Michael, it's just not," Joy responded. She still felt badly that she couldn't remember her time spent with him. Michael could see his question made her sad.

"Hey, it's okay...don't worry, it will," he assured her.

Michael got out of the car, walked around to Joy's door and opened it for her. He extended his hand towards her. Joy reached out and grabbed Michael's hand.

They walked toward the sanctuary entrance. Joy looked around at all of the vegetation and then she saw a family of ducks waddle out from behind a bush. A mother duck and seven little babies.

"Oh look!" she said excitedly. "I think I will name them."

"Haha, you already did. See, you will remember," he said.

The ducks came closer to Joy and seemed to feel safe around her. She couldn't believe a mother duck would allow her babies so close to a human.

"They want you to feed them like you always do," Michael explained as he pulled a bag of duck pellets from his jacket pocket. He passed the bag of food to Joy.

"Here ya go, you feed them," he said.

Joy looked down at the bag of duck food, "Thanks!"

She knelt down by the ducks and gently tossed the food in their direction. They all fluttered over to gobble it up.

"Awww, poor little guy isn't getting any," she said as she tossed more toward the runt in the group.

"Pee-wee, is his name pee-wee?" she asked Michael.

"But of course!" he answered.

Joy giggled and continued to feed the ducks. When the food was all gone they entered the wildlife sanctuary and walked down a beautiful path. There were little chipmunks darting around, squirrels clinging to trees and birds everywhere. Occasionally she would see a wild rabbit hop by.

He walked her to an area where you could view the wild deer. Michael stopped and turned to face Joy. He grabbed both her hands, looked her in the eyes and got down on one knee.

"You are the love of my life and no one could make me happier. Will you marry me?" he asked.

Joy was surprised and confused, "What?"

"This is the spot where I asked you to be my wife and you said yes," he told her.

"Ohhh," she smiled and blushed.

"You didn't answer me and my knees aren't getting any younger," Michael joked.

"Yes, silly," Joy laughed as she pulled him up towards her. Michael looked her in the eyes and moved closer to kiss her. They embraced each other and Joy felt wonderful.   She didn't want this feeling to end so she held onto him as long as she could.

They walked around the sanctuary for a couple of hours talking and enjoying nature. Michael shared things about himself and memories that he thought they shared. Joy was glad to be learning so much about him and about who she was in this place. She was finding out that she was pretty much the same in this life as she was in the real life, only this life was turning out to be much better.

After a long day of seeing the island and their favorite places Michael drove Joy home. They pulled into the driveway to see Patricia driving away. She waved and Michael waved back. When they arrived home they found the house smelling delicious.

Patricia had made them a nice warm meal at Micheal's request. And when they walked into the house all of the rooms were lit by romantic candlelight.

"My Mother has good timing," he told Joy.

"What do you mean?" she asked.

"I asked her to come over and have this dinner ready for us. It was the same dinner we ate the night of our engagement. I thought recreating a few memories might help you," he explained.

"I sure am enjoying these memories, new or old they are just perfect," she said lovingly.

Michael and Joy spent the entire day together and it was the most romantic day she had ever experienced. All too soon it was time to go to bed. Joy didn't want to go to sleep. She was afraid she would wake up in the real world again. She closed her eyes and made a wish.

Chapter Ten

When Joy opened her eyes the next day, she was still on Goose Island. She was still laying in the bed next to Michael and his arms were still wrapped around her. She couldn't help notice how adorable he was as he slept. She even thought the few little gray hairs poking through made him look more handsome. His five o'clock shadow was sexy she thought. He looked youthful for his age and his smile was intoxicating.

It was a strange feeling to know that she was married to this man but he was a stranger to her. Oddly enough she was experiencing strong feelings for Michael. Although she hadn't really known him very long, she felt like she did.

Joy's enchantment was soon disrupted when she locked eyes with Honey. Honey had her leash in her mouth and was dragging it as she was trotting toward the bed.

"No, no, no.." she whispered sternly hoping Honey would listen. She suddenly knew it was too late. Honey leaped on the bed and jumped right on top of Joy and Michael.

"AHHH!" Michael yelled, "Honey get down!"

Honey jumped off the bed and sat with her leash dangling from her mouth staring at Michael sadly.

"I guess it's time to walk Honey. I'll take her this time," Michael said as he sat up stretching. Michael got dressed and gave Joy a kiss. He hooked the leash to Honey's collar.

"I'll be back soon," he told Joy. "Maybe you'd like to get familiar with the kitchen and make us some breakfast?"

"Ummm...okay," she answered.

Michael left with Honey. Joy got up and noticed a rocking chair in the corner of the bedroom. She hadn't noticed it before, but she was still taking in a lot of information. She walked over to examine it closer. It was exactly like the rocking chair she had at home. It was a rocking chair that was brought over on the boat from Wales by her ancestors and it was over five hundred years old. It even had the exact same wear and tear.

"Well it is MY daydream, so I guess it makes sense that would be here," she thought to herself.

Joy loved that rocking chair it was the only family heirloom that she had. Since both her parents were deceased this was extremely important to her. This rocker carried a lot of emotional value to Joy. She smiled and was happy it was here. After she got dressed she pranced out of the room and down the stairs.

"I wonder if I can bring Fitch and the fish here?" she thought silently. "If I could bring my pets here, I'd have no real reason to go home."

She began to concentrate and focus on her pets and tried to visualize them living with her on Goose Island in her beach home. She closed her eyes and thought about Fitch she peeked one eye open but no kitty. She closed her eyes tightly and thought about the fish. She opened her eyes but nothing had changed.

"Here kitty, kitty, come here Fitch!" she called, but Fitch didn't come.

She stood in the kitchen looking around and opened the refrigerator. It was packed full of delicious food. She opened the freezer and it was packed too. She began to get bacon and eggs out of the refrigerator when the doorbell rang. She set the food down on the counter and went to answer the door.

Joy opened the door, it was Dr. Lewis. He was smiling when she opened the door and he looked just as handsome as she remembered. He was closer to Joy's age and very fit. He was dressed in his jogging clothes and his skin glistened with perspiration.

"Good morning, Joy. Is Michael home?" Dr. Lewis asked.

"No, he took Honey for a walk. I'm not sure when he'll be back," she answered as she started to shut the door.

Dr. Lewis put his hand on the door to stop her from shutting it. "He usually walks her up the beach near my house. He'll be gone a while. Anyhow, I'm here to see you. You didn't come to my office the other day and I was worried about you," he told her.

His eyes pierced through her with a look like he knew her more intimately. She had never really been good at reading people so she doubted this feeling. When she was in college in the real world she thought her handsome dorm brother Todd was winking at her. It turned out he just wore contacts and was having problems with them. So she dismissed this thought about Dr. Lewis with no concern.

"I'm married and deeply in love with Michael anyhow, right?" she thought. "I'm not a promiscuous person anyhow."

Dr. Lewis smiled, "May I come in?"

"Oh sure, I was just going to make breakfast," she replied.

Dr. Lewis placed his hand in the small of her back and Joy felt a tingle through her entire body. She quickly stepped away, although she didn't want to.

"Joy, I really need you to come to my office today so I can have a look at you and run a few tests. I'm concerned about you," he told her.

"I'm fine, really I'm just...just fine," she told him.

"You aren't acting quite like yourself yet and you look a little pale. I think we should check your iron levels at the very least," he urged.

"Well..." Joy hesitated.

"Are you still having those dizzy spells?" he asked.

"I haven't had one in a few days," Joy answered.

He leaned in and looked deeply into Joy's eyes. She began to feel something for him again. A part of her thought that it really didn't matter since this was merely a daydream.

"But what if it's real?" she thought.

Dr. Lewis was gazing deeply into her eyes when he suddenly said, "Yep, your color is a little off."

He stepped away and Joy thought, "Huh? I read him wrong. He *really* is just concerned about my health."

"Joy, I can't stress enough how important it is that you come to my office today and get checked out. If you don't then I can't be held liable for what happens to you," he told her sternly.

"Okay, I will," she insisted.

"Promise me," he said.

"I promise, I'll be there," she said reluctantly as she led him to the door.

"Okay, well Michael should be back shortly. I have to finish my run and get to work. I will see you in a little while," Dr. Lewis waved at Joy as he jogged away.

As Dr. Lewis jogged away a little red Volkswagen Beetle pulled into their driveway and up to the house. The car had rust spots in several areas and her front bumper was dented. There was a heavy set woman driving the car. She was approximately in her thirties and had her dirty blonde hair pulled back in a pony tail. Some of her hair was sticking out the sides in a messy fashion. She waved and smiled at Joy.

Joy waved back tilting her head curiously wondering, "Who is she?"

The woman struggled to get out of her car due to her weight issues. As she exited the vehicle Joy noticed she was dressed in black yoga pants and a stained sweatshirt.

"Can I help you?" Joy asked as she stepped outside onto the porch and came down the steps.

"Where have you been? You haven't returned any of my calls all week. Is your answering machine broken? Look at you! You are letting yourself go. I see you've put on a few pounds," the large woman told Joy.

"I'm sorry- I have lost some memories. Who are you?" Joy asked.

"Oh, you poor thing! What happened?" she asked.

"I guess I hit my head on some rocks or something down at the beach, umm I don't really know. Ummm who are you?" Joy asked again.

"Sweetie, I'm your life coach and fitness instructor! My name is Beth," she told her. "You've missed your last three appointments with me."

Joy looked her up and down and couldn't help but notice the irony. Beth stood in front of her weighing probably three or maybe even four times the weight of Joy. And yes, Joy had noticed she had put on a few pounds but it was nothing compared to this woman's problems. Beth had messy hair, a junky car, stained clothes and if Joy had met her on the street she would have thought she was a homeless person.

"I haven't been quite myself lately," Joy told Beth.

"Joy, you better get in and see the doctor," Beth said with concern.

"Yes, it seems everyone has been telling me that lately, including Dr. Lewis," Joy responded. "In fact, I'm going to see him today."

Just then Michael came walking up with Honey. Honey started barking at Beth and wagging her tail. Michael took Honey up the front steps and let her in the house.

"Hey Beth, what's up?" Michael asked as he walked toward Joy and Beth.

"I've been leaving messages for Joy and she's missed her last three appointments with me. I thought I had better stop by and see if everything was alright," Beth told him.

"She hasn't been well and she probably won't be able to get in to see you for a while," he told her. Joy got the impression that Michael didn't really like Beth.

"Joy," Beth leaned in to speak quietly so Michael wouldn't hear. "Could you maybe advance me my next month of pay. I've got some bills," her voice dropped lower as she spoke.

"I would be glad to help, but I don't even know where my checkbook or purse is right now," Joy said compassionately.

"I could drive you to the art gallery and you could just get me some cash from the cash register," Beth told her.

Michael interrupted, "Look Beth, I know you need some cash. Here," he said as he pulled a wad of cash from his wallet. "Please don't come up here and bother my wife for a while. She's needs some time to get her thoughts together. She will call you when she is ready to see you."

"Thanks, Michael," Beth said as she took the cash and put her head down in shame. "Joy, I'll see you soon I hope. If you need anything just call me," her disposition changed as Joy smiled at her. She turned and got into her car and drove away. The car blew smoke out of the exhaust as she accelerated.

"I don't know why you pay that woman," Michael said as he turned toward Joy.

"I don't either," Joy smirked. "Is she really my life coach and fitness instructor?"

Michael smiled, "I keep forgetting that you don't remember everything. Yes, she is a life coach and fitness instructor. It's not her calling if you ask me."

"You gotta hand it to her. She's got confidence!" Joy laughed.

"Not really," Michael explained, "She secretly goes to counseling twice a week for depression but everyone in town knows. But for some strange reason you and several other people take her advice and go to her fitness classes. I just don't get it."

"Maybe she's doing something right. I am quite successful, right?" Joy asked.

"You know you are," Michael told her as he wrapped his arms around her. "Let's go eat breakfast. I can't wait to see what you made."

"BREAKFAST!" Joy slapped the palm of her hand to her forehead. "The doctor stopped over and then..."

"The doctor?" Michael asked. "What did he want?"

"I was supposed to have some tests done at his office a few days ago and I haven't been in to see him. He wants me to come in today and I told him I would," Joy answered.

"I will come with you, but let's go make breakfast together first," Michael told her in a nurturing tone. They walked with spirited steps into the house hand in hand.

Chapter Eleven

Joy sat in the sterile office staring at the chart of the human body on the wall. The little paper gown didn't cover much and the office was chilly. She wasn't finding this enjoyable and thought it was an odd thing to have in her daydream. She tried to think pleasant thoughts and to change her current experience.

She thought about her home and the beach, "I'd rather be walking on the beach than sitting here," she mumbled.

"Me too!" said Dr. Lewis as the door swung open and startled Joy.

"I was just..." Joy tried to explain.

"Talking to yourself," he finished her sentence. "I know, I do that too quite often."

He held her chart in his hands and looked at her quite intently. Joy began to fidget nervously.

"It's not bad enough to be sitting here half naked in front of a handsome stranger," she thought silently, "but what is he going to tell me? He's already run several tests on me. Is he going to run more? He looks very serious, maybe I *do* have a brain tumor."

"Is that Michael in my waiting room?" he asked her.

"Yes," Joy answered.

"Would you like him to come in to hear the results?" Dr. Lewis asked.

Joy thought how it would be nice to have Michael there to comfort her if the news turned out bad. She nodded.

"I'll have the nurse go get him," Dr. Lewis said.

He stepped out of the room briefly to talk to the nurse. The suspense was killing her.

"Why am I here?" she thought. "I could be doing this in the real world. Why would I choose to do this to myself in my fantasy world when I could be doing *anything* else? I need to work harder on controlling my thoughts."

Michael and Dr. Lewis entered the room. Michael stepped over next to Joy and put his arm around her. Dr. Lewis opened her chart.

"You've had dizzy spells, which your Mother in law expressed to me she thought was due to you hitting your head. The tests reveal something quite different," the doctor told her. "In fact, the dizzy spells may have caused you to fall and hit your head."

"Okay, get on with it," Michael told him impatiently. "What's wrong with her?"

"Joy, you're pregnant," Dr. Lewis told her.

Joy felt dizzy again and room spun out of control. Then everything went black.

"Joy, Joy!! are you alright," asked Paul.

Joy opened her eyes to her dismay to see her co-worker Paul patting her cheek with his hand trying to wake her up. She was laying on the floor in the meeting room surrounded by all of her co-workers, her supervisor, and the boss. Everyone was looking down at her.

"Paul?" Joy said in a groggy voice.

As she scanned the faces in the crowd she saw many concerned expressions. Some people looked irritated at her. She wondered why. She felt embarrassed. A paramedic entered the room moments later.

"Everyone step back and give us some room," the paramedic told them.

Everyone moved out of the way and the paramedic knelt down next to Joy and began checking her vitals and asking her questions. Joy still felt a little dazed and confused but she was coming to her senses.

After the paramedic checked her vitals and spoke to her, she declined to be taken away in the ambulance. The paramedic went over to speak to her boss in private. She couldn't hear what they were saying but she didn't like their body language. The paramedic shook his head and her boss waved his hands around a bit as if he were upset.

"Are you alright, Joy?" asked Tanya, another co-worker.

"I'm fine. Why am I on the floor? What happened?" she whispered to Tanya.

"We were in the middle of the meeting and you looked sleepy and then you just fell out of your chair and passed out. That's it. You might have bumped your head. Then Paul was closest to you so he was trying to wake you up and the boss called the ambulance," Tanya told her quietly.

"Help me stand up," Joy told her.

Tanya grabbed her hand and helped her get on her feet. Joy still felt a little woozy but she put on a good act to look normal. The boss saw Tanya help her up.

"Don't touch her!" the boss yelled at Tanya.

He walked over to Joy, she was on her feet, "Joy, I really think you should go with the paramedic to the hospital and get checked out."

"No, I'm fine," she insisted. "I just need a drink of water."

"Then I need to speak to you privately. Come to my office," the boss told her firmly. "Someone get her a bottle of water!" he shouted at the others in the room. "..and the rest of you get back to work!"

Olivia stood in the corner sneering at Joy. Another female co-worker brought Joy a bottle of water. Joy sat down and drank the water. After she felt composed she went to see the boss. She knocked gently on his door.

"Come in!" he said sharply. "Sit down."

"Look, I know it looks..." Joy started to try to explain that she was alright.

"Normally I wouldn't want to know what is going on with you, but when something is happening that affects the company, then I need to know. Your production here at work has been down for several months and now you are falling asleep in meetings?" He asked.

109

"I just haven't been getting enough sleep and I haven't been falling asleep in meetings plural. It was one meeting," she told him. If was the first time she ever thought of defending herself at work.

"If it keeps up then we'll have to let you go. You should probably see a doctor, you look awful," the boss responded.

"I've been meaning to go to a doctor..." she started saying.

"Well, just do it!" snapped the boss.

"Okay, I will," she said quietly.

"I want you to go home and get some rest and I expect you back here on Monday. You'll have to use some sick leave or vacation time, that's what it's there for, you know," he added.

"I've already used up all of my sick days and vacation time," Joy told him.

The boss scribbled something on a piece of paper, "Here, take this to human resources and they'll let you have time off with no pay."

"Oh wonderful," she thought to herself. "Just what I need, Mr. Big-spender over there thinks he's doing me a favor. I'll be racking up a doctor bill and losing money from work."

Joy took the paper and thanked her boss politely and walked out of his office. She went downstairs to the human resource department and handed Mrs. Henderson the slip.

"Here, the boss said to give this to you," Joy told her.

Mrs. Henderson looked at the slip, "Wow! You're lucky," and she meant it. "Mr. Wilson never lets people take unpaid leave. I've been asking for extra time off for twenty years. What did you do to get this?"

"I fell asleep in a meeting," Joy answered.

"Geez if I had known I just needed to fall asleep at work to get extra time off, I would have done it a long time ago!" Mrs. Henderson was quite serious.

Joy rolled her eyes, "Yeah a whole day off with no pay, I should be grateful, huh?"

Mrs. Henderson looked at her angrily and handed her a document to sign. She took it back stamped it and handed her a copy. Mrs. Henderson mumbled something to herself about what a darn shame it was to have lazy workers getting the benefits she felt she deserved. She typed up some paperwork as Joy waited tensely.

"Can I go now?" Joy asked.

"Oh yes, you can go. We'll see you back here Monday. Enjoy your weekend." Mrs. Henderson said with some jealousy in her voice.

Joy *was* glad to have an extended weekend, but she knew this wouldn't be a resolution to the bigger problems.

Joy sent a text message to Julie and Nicole to let them know what had happened. Nicole offered to give her a lift to the doctor, but Joy declined. Joy agreed to meet Julie at a coffee shop.

Joy sat alone at the table in the coffee shop waiting for Julie to arrive. She was late and Joy was on her second mocha latte. The cookies were starting to look pretty good. So it was a good thing Julie walked in when she did, but she wasn't alone. She was dangling on Eric's arm.

Joy saw them, "Oh no, she brought Eric. Why did she bring him?" she thought silently but smiled at both of them.

"Hey girl!" Julie said.

"Hi, hon," Joy answered.

Julie could already see from the look that Joy was giving her that Eric wasn't welcome in this conversation.

"Eric arrived at my door just as I was leaving and offered to drive me here," Julie explained.

"Hi Eric, I'm Joy it's nice to meet you," Joy told him.

"Hi nice to meet you too," he extended his hand to shake Joy's.

"Could you be a sweetheart and go get me a vanilla latte?" Julie told Eric.

"Sure babe," Eric answered.

As soon as Eric was out of earshot Julie told Joy, "Look I'll make this quick. This is the phone number for that doctor Nicole said you should see. I think she might be right. Don't get me wrong, I think it's great this whole other world you've imagined or whatever it is. But just to be safe you better get checked out. Here take this." Julie handed Joy the paper with the phone number for the doctor. Joy tucked the paper in her purse.

"I know," Joy said sullenly. "When I left Goose Island the doctor there just told me that I'm pregnant."

"What!?" Julie shrieked. "what?" she said softer looking around to see if anyone was listening.

"On Goose Island I am pregnant and now I'm worried I could be pregnant here too. Remember the cut on my finger?" Joy told her.

"But how could you be? You haven't been with anyone in months, right?" Julie asked.

"Yes, it's been a while," Joy answered. "But I'm gaining weight and feeling dizzy and I passed out at work today."

"Look, I'll ditch Eric and then stop at the pharmacy and get you a pregnancy test. I'll meet you at your house later, okay?" Julie asked.

"Alright, I'll see you at my house. I'm supposed to go home and get some rest anyhow," Joy told her.

Just then Eric came back to the table with two coffees in to go cups and handed one to Julie. He smiled at Julie and gave her a peck on the cheek.

"You know, we should just take these and go," she told Eric rushing him out the door. "I forgot I have some errands to run and things to do, so if you could just drop me back off at my place..." her voice faded as they exited the coffee shop.

Joy sat there for a moment thinking about her situation. She was really frightened now. But she knew what she had to do next.

Chapter Twelve

Joy paced anxiously back and forth in her living room.
Fitch followed her like a shadow. The cat weaved in and
out between her legs nearly tripping her as she walked.
Joy would only stop pacing to peek out the living room
window. She was supposed to come home and get some
rest, but who could rest thinking about such things. Her
anxiety was overwhelming her.

"Where is Julie? What's taking her so long?" Joy
said out loud.

She tried to meditate but she couldn't calm her
mind. Joy turned on the television to try and drown out
her thoughts, but her thoughts would not leave her alone.
She turned the television off. Then came a frantic knock
on the door.

"It's me! Sorry I took so long," Julie told her
through the door.

Joy opened the door quickly, "Oh thank God you are here. I've been going nuts waiting. I couldn't rest at all."

"I had a hard time getting Eric to let me *run errands* alone. I'll tell you, he's great but a little too clingy," Julie explained.

Julie handed Joy the pharmacy bag. Joy ripped it open and ran to the bathroom. She fumbled with the box and was trying to read the instructions too fast.

"What's wrong in there?" Julie asked.

"Ugh! I'm trying to read the instructions!" Joy said in frustration as she stepped back into the living room.

"You just pee on the stick!" Julie told her.

"Have you used these before?" Joy asked.

"Oh yeah. I've had a few pregnancy scares. Those are really easy to use," Julie answered.

Joy took the package back into the bathroom. A few moments later she came out of the bathroom a little more relaxed and said, "Now we wait."

The two girls had plenty to talk about but neither could breathe a word right now. They sat in awkward silence. The timer went off and Joy bolted off the couch.

"It's time!" Joy cried out.

Joy ran into the bathroom to check the stick. She was in there for a moment and then walked out slowly holding the pregnancy test. She showed Julie the positive result.

"No! What?! Seriously?!" Julie was stunned.

Joy flopped onto the couch and Julie sat down beside her. Joy got tears in her eyes and turned to look at Julie. A tear trickled down Joy's cheek and Julie wiped it away and gave Joy a hug. Julie knew Joy very well and knew she'd never lie to her, but even she was having a hard time believing Joy's story at this moment. A cloud of doubt floated through Julie's mind.

"Joy, are you sure you are being completely honest with me?" Julie asked hesitantly.

"I can't believe you just asked me that. You are closer to me than anyone I know. We tell each other everything, I mean *everything*!" Joy retaliated.

"I know, I'm sorry. It's just such a difficult thing to understand. Forget I said that," Julie apologized and hugged her again. "I'm so very sorry."

Joy pulled away from Julie and looked her in the face, "You do realize what this means?"

"It's REAL! Goose Island is real! It's not your daydream. Do you think it's an alternate universe and you travel through a wormhole or something or..." Julie said with excitement.

117

"What do I look like, a scientist or quantum physicist?" Joy answered. "I thought I was controlling it until I ended up in that doctor's office. That was when a part of me realized it might not be just a daydream."

Julie was still thinking about the alternate universe theory, "no, if it were an alternate universe there would have to be another you, right?"

"Will you stop talking about alternate universes and science. I'm pregnant. I need to go see a doctor," Joy told her.

"You're right. What are you going to tell the doctor?" Julie asked.

"I'm just going to tell him I'm pregnant. He doesn't need to know much more than that," Joy told replied.

"You should probably call your doctor now to get an appointment. It's hard to get an appointment on a Friday," Julie told her.

Joy looked at the clock, "Yeah, I guess there's still a little time to call." She picked up her cell phone and called her regular doctor. After speaking to the receptionist on the phone she looked at Julie.

"Are they getting you in?" Julie asked.

"Yes, it turns out it's not my doctor's weekend to play golf," she laughed. "I have an appointment tomorrow afternoon."

"Do you want me to stay with you tonight and go there with you tomorrow?" Julie asked.

"I think I'd like that," Joy answered.

"I'll just run home and get an overnight bag and I'll be back in a little while," Julie hugged Joy. Then Joy laid down to take a nap.

While Julie was out gathering her things to stay at Joy's house she thought she should keep Nicole in the loop.

She called Nicole on her phone, "Nicole?"

"Yeah, what's going on?" Nicole asked. She sounded busy, but she always sounded busy.

"I was just with Joy. I need to bring you up to speed on everything." Julie informed her.

"Okay, what happened? Is she okay?" she asked.

"Long story short- Joy was on Goose Island again. She met Michael and she found out she is pregnant," Julie told her.

"Wait, she's pregnant?" Nicole interjected.

"Yes, but it started on Goose Island and now she's pregnant here," Julie went on.

"Do you know how ridiculous you sound?" Nicole asked her. "How can that even be!?"

"I know, I even doubted it for a moment, but I know Joy and she wouldn't lie to me. She tells me everything. So this means it's an alternate universe or something," Julie told her.

"No, it means that our friend is sick. She's probably got a split personality or something and you are buying into her story," Nicole insisted.

"Then how do you explain the pregnancy? She hasn't even dated a guy in several months!" Julie defended Joy.

"No, it means her other personality has been with a guy and didn't tell her. She's in some serious trouble and we've got to get her in to a doctor immediately," Nicole sounded upset.

"Don't worry she has an appointment with her regular doctor tomorrow," Julie said hoping to give Nicole some peace of mind.

"Her regular doctor, I guess that's a start. She needs to see a mental health professional," Nicole said judgmentally.

"I'm going with her tomorrow and I'll keep an eye on her tonight. Don't you think we would have seen a guy hanging around or some signs of a guy if she were seeing someone?" Julie questioned.

"Maybe not, I've been doing some reading on the matter since Joy told us about all of this. Her other personality can be sneaky. It could be a person completely unlike Joy. She could be going out and doing things that Joy would never think of doing," Nicole explained.

"Do you really think that's what's happening?" Julie asked. Julie began to feel concerned again.

"I don't know, but I can't think of any other reasonable explanation. Unless you think our friend is just a flat out liar," Nicole stated bluntly.

"I *know* she's not that. I'll tell you what. I'm staying the night at her house tonight. I'll look around for signs of a man, you know like an extra toothbrush, a razor or any kind of evidence of a man being there. If I find *anything* I will let you know right away," Julie said.

"A baby inside her is plenty of proof of a man and, like I told you her other personality could be hiding things from the Joy we know and love. I wouldn't expect you to find anything. If you want to look around or happen to see something then, sure let me know," Nicole told her.

"I will," she said.

"Did you give her that phone number for the doctor I suggested?" Nicole asked.

"Yes, she has it. I spoke to her briefly but with the shock of the pregnancy we didn't talk too much about that doctor," Julie answered.

"Okay well I was finishing some work when you called, so I'll have to talk to you later," Nicole told her.

"Alright, bye," Julie ended the call.

Julie finished packing her overnight bag and contemplated if Nicole could be right. She cared deeply for her best friend Joy and wanted what was best for her. She just didn't know what to think anymore.

The next day Julie drove Joy to the doctor's office. She had done her snooping around Joy's house and didn't find any proof of a man being around. It didn't mean that Joy hadn't been seeing a man some place else. Julie didn't feel good about looking through her best friend's things. She just kept telling herself it was for the good of Joy.

The women approached the doctor's office. The office door had the doctor's name, DR. YU PAEMEMOR, in big shiny gold letters.   She had been seeing this doctor for several years and had built a relationship of trust with her doctor.

They sat in the waiting room and every time Julie tried to talk about Goose Island Joy would shush her. She didn't want someone to overhear.   Joy told Julie they'd discuss it later. So, they sat there quietly and anxiously waiting to be called back.

Eventually it was Joy's turn and the nurse came out and called her name. Julie followed her back to the exam room. Her weight was up ten pounds from her last visit.

"What's the purpose of your visit today?" the nurse asked.

"Like I said on the phone, I took a home pregnancy test and it was positive," Joy answered. Joy hated the repetitive questions that are asked when you see a doctor. You have to tell them on the phone, then you have to tell the nurse and finally the doctor asks the same questions.

"It has to be on my chart," she thought silently as she grew more irritated.

"Oh! Congratulations!" the nurse told her.

Joy tried to act happy but she was really nervous. She dodged the nurses questions about the baby's father. They made small talk as the nurse took her vital signs and noted her chart. Julie sat in the corner silent, but wanting to say something. The nurse told them the doctor would be in shortly and she put Joy's chart on the door and left.

Dr. Paememor entered the room. He was an older Asian man with flecks of gray in his black hair. He wore his wire rimmed glasses on the tip of his nose. The doctor's mother was Asian and his father was born in the states. He was born in the states as well. When Joy first started seeing this doctor she was concerned he wouldn't speak English very well. She was relieved that he did. There's nothing like going to a doctor for something as crucial as your health and well being and not understanding what they are saying. Dr. Paememor had proven to be an excellent doctor that Joy trusted completely.

"Hello Joy. What brings you here today?"

"Like I told your nurse, I'm pregnant," Joy answered with a bit of snap in her voice. She grumbled to herself about his redundant questions.

"And how do you know you are pregnant?" he asked.

"I took a home pregnancy test," she answered.

He asked all of the personal questions that doctors ask in that situation. Joy answered them all as honestly as she could.

"We'll do a little blood work and have you go pee in a cup. Then I'll be back in to talk to you," said Dr. Paememor.

After all the blood was drawn and the tests were done the doctor came back in the room. He had a serious look on his face. Joy and Julie both took notice and wondered what was wrong.

"Joy, I will cut to the chase here. The tests show you are not pregnant. You must have gotten a false positive on the home pregnancy test. I am concerned though about your weight gain, your dizzy spells, your fatigue and you seem a little depressed," he told her.

Both women were shocked at what he said, "It can't be," Joy said.

"It happens more often than you would think. These home kits are not always reliable. Are you stressed?" asked Dr. Paememor. He glanced over Joy's shoulder at Julie who was nodding frantically. He could tell she wanted to say something. Julie was beginning to feel like Nicole was right.

"I have been a little stressed, but mostly tired," Joy answered.

"It says on your chart both of your parents are deceased. When did they pass?" the doctor asked.

"A little over a year ago. They were in a car accident," Joy answered.

"Hmmm...did you get any counseling for this?" he prodded.

"No," Joy answered.

"I think it would benefit you to see a counselor because it sounds like you are still grieving. The stress is an obvious result of losing both your parents suddenly," the doctor told her.

"I guess," said Joy.

"And how is work?" the doctor asked.

"She hates her job," Julie blurted out.

Joy glared at Julie, but she held her tongue.

"I would definitely say between work and the loss of your parents, that you are struggling with depression," said Dr. Paememor.

"When you leave, the ladies at the desk can set up an appointment with a mental health doctor," he told her. He handed her some papers and ushered her out of the room. Julie started to follow but stopped. When she saw Joy was busy speaking to the receptionist she grabbed the doctor's arm.

"Do you have something to tell me?" the doctor asked.

"Yes, but in private," she whispered.

The doctor motioned her back toward the exam room.

"Joy, I'm just going to use the ladies room," Julie yelled across the room. Joy nodded and went back to talking to the woman at the desk.

126

The doctor closed the door of the exam room, "So, what was it that you wanted to tell me?" asked the doctor.

"Joy doesn't have any family since her parents died. She's not very social lately and is very withdrawn. Nicole and I are like her family. We are concerned about her...oh I shouldn't be telling you this," Julie stopped. She was conflicted. She felt like she was betraying her best friend.

"No, go on," said Dr. Paememor.

"Our friend Nicole suspects Julie might have a split personality disorder. I don't think so but..." Julie paused.

"What makes her think this?" the doctor asked.

"Well, I just wanted to know if stress could cause that?" asked Julie. "I've known Joy since we were kids and she's never...." Julie stopped again.

"Don't worry. I'll put it in her chart to have the mental health doctor watch for signs. If she does have this disorder then he will get to the bottom of it. If it's just stress or depression then he is qualified to diagnose that as well and treat her."

Julie thanked him and quickly went looking for Joy before she decided to come looking for her.

Chapter Thirteen

The doctor made sure Joy got an appointment to see the mental health counselor the following week. She had to adjust her schedule at work and it wasn't easy since her boss was not very cooperative. Joy arrived promptly to see Dr. Vanderstein. She wasn't eager to discuss anything personal and especially not anxious to share her travels to Goose Island.

She was beginning to wonder if she would go back to the island. She hadn't been there since Thursday when she fell asleep at the meeting. She did sleep a lot over the weekend and gained another two pounds.

Joy completed the forms as she sat in Dr. Vanderstein's lobby. She waited for them to call her back. She didn't really lie on the forms but she left out a lot of details.

At a quarter after the hour, the receptionist finally told her she could go in. The doctor was not any more punctual than her regular doctor.

"Come in and make yourself comfortable, I'm Dr. Vanderstein. It's nice to meet you, Joy," he told her.

Joy sat down in an over stuffed chair. It looked comfortable but it was deceiving. The chair gobbled her up so her feet didn't touch the floor and she felt like a child. She assumed this was done purposely to make the patient feel more vulnerable.

The doctor studied her for a moment, which made Joy feel even more awkward. She could see he was sizing her up. She watched his eyes as they looked at the placement of her hands and her body language.

"Well, let's see. It says here your parents passed away about a year ago?" he read from her chart.

"That's correct," she told him.

"Let's start there. Tell me about your parents," said Dr. Vanderstein.

"I loved my parents very much and I miss them every day. Mom and Dad were high school sweethearts. I was an only child. Mom did have a miscarriage before me, it was a boy," she told the doctor.

"Your parents decided not to have any more children?" the doctor asked.

"Mom had difficulty with my pregnancy and birth. They did try for a while but ultimately decided it was not healthy for Mom or another child," Joy answered as she watched the doctor jot down notes.

"Tell me about their passing, they were young," the doctor prodded.

"Yes. The day it happened I was at work. They had left that day to take a mini vacation and drive up the coast. They had just got on the highway and ..." Joy choked up and tears welled up in her eyes.

"Here," the doctor said as he handed her some tissue.

She wiped her tears and cleared her throat, "...another driver was texting. I got the call pretty early in the morning. The hospital called and told me that my mother died at the scene of the accident but Dad was in critical condition. I rushed out of work and don't remember the drive at all. Dad lingered for three days, he looked awful. At least he was unconscious."

Joy went silent. Dr. Vanderstein looked at her chart again and this time he noticed the special note Dr. Paememor added. He raised one eyebrow with curiosity but, he didn't say anything.

"Okay, so why did you go see Dr. Paememor?" he asked her.

"I thought I was pregnant," she told him.

"Oh, you are married?" he asked.

"No," she replied.

"Then you have a boyfriend, can you tell me about your relationship?" he asked.

"No, I'm not seeing anyone," she told him.

"Well then tell me about your last relationship, the one you thought fathered your child," he persisted.

Joy didn't know what to say. She didn't want to tell him the truth but, knew if she didn't say something he would know she was hiding something.

"I- I haven't been with anyone for a while," she said reluctantly.

"Hmmm, I guess I'm a little confused then. Why did you think you were pregnant?" He asked.

"I gained weight, I was having dizzy spells and I took a home pregnancy test. The test came back positive, but the lab results from the doctor came back negative," she told him.

"Alright, but am I understanding you haven't been intimate with anyone in a while?" he asked.

Joy got nervous but tried not to fidget, she knew he was watching her body language. "Umm I mean, no," said Joy tensely. "I just don't want to talk about him," Joy said trying to cover her tracks.

"How long has it been?" he asked.

"Several months," she told him. "I mean..." Joy wasn't a good liar and it was obvious.

The doctor paused to think. Joy was growing increasingly anxious. She clamped her hands together in her lap. Her entire body got tense. The doctor noticed the bandage on her finger.

"What happened to your hand?" he asked.

"I cut it," she told him.

"*You* cut it?" he asked.

"I m-mean it was an accident," she stammered. "I broke a glass and cut it picking up the glass."

The doctor sensed Joy was hiding something.

"I think it would be a good idea to do some testing and then when the testing is done we'll continue this conversation another day," he told her. "The receptionist will schedule for a day of testing and your follow up appointment."

"Doctor, I really don't think I need..." Joy started.

"There's nothing for you to be concerned about. I'm just here to help you. If we can target the problem then we can help you get better sleep and feel less stressed," persisted Dr. Vanderstein.

Joy had a knot in her stomach. She felt like her gut was telling her this was not in her best interest, but she didn't follow her gut. Instead, she set up the appointments to come back for testing and a follow up appointment.

After Joy left the office Dr. Vanderstein decided to contact Dr. Paememor about Joy's chart. He wanted to know more about the special notes on the chart.

"Hello Yu? This is Dr. Carl Vanderstein calling about the patient you referred to me. The depression case with the false pregnancy, Joy..."

"Oh yes, Carl, how can I help you," asked Yu.

"What is this note about possible multiple personality disorder?" asked Dr. Vanderstein.

"Her friend came in with her last week. She was really worried about Joy and she suggested it but didn't go into details," he answered.

"How did she suggest it?" Carl asked.

"She mentioned it but didn't indicate why she had that impression. I decided to drop a note on the chart to alert you there *could* be a problem." answered Yu.

"What do you think?" Carl asked.

"That's not my area of expertise. That's why I referred her to you. I noticed signs of depression and thought it would be wise to refer her out to counseling," Yu told him.

"How long has she been your patient? I mean, how well do you know her?" asked Dr. Vanderstein.

"She's been coming here for years and hasn't exhibited anything out of the ordinary if that's what you're asking," answered Dr. Paememor.

"I guess I find it odd that she thought she was pregnant and she hasn't been intimate with anyone in several months, so she says," explained Dr. Vanderstein.

"Hmmm, she didn't express that to me," said Dr. Paememor. "Are you certain you understood her correctly?"

"Quite certain but, I'm having her come in for an extensive psych evaluation. If I misunderstood in anyway it will come out in the testing," explained Dr. Vanderstein. "Thanks for your time."

"No problem," said Yu.

Dr. Vanderstein hung up and moved on to his next patient.

Joy returned to work immediately after her appointment. She had missed her lunch and had to sneak some snacks at her desk. She felt like everyone was watching her now. She could hear whispering and co-workers looking at her differently. She wished she felt invisible again.

This was turning into one of the longest days of her life. She couldn't stop worrying about what kinds of psychological testing would be done. She felt like she really screwed things up when she told her doctor that she hadn't been dating. She was worried, afraid, and felt chained to her desk. She wanted to crawl into a hole and never come out.

Joy's boss came over to her desk, "How are you feeling?" he asked.

"Fine," Joy answered and started typing. She didn't feel like talking to him or anyone else at work.

"Okay, well let us know if there are any problems," the boss told her and walked away. He acted like he cared but Joy knew he was just putting on a show.

Joy turned her thoughts to Goose Island. It was the only place she felt safe these days. However, she wasn't quite sure what to think about being pregnant there. It was a lot to take in. She was beginning to wish that she could just live that life and never come back to her real life. But now she was contemplating which life was her real life.

The more time she spent on the island the more real it felt and the more difficult it was to keep secret. She constantly found herself nearly saying something to someone about Michael, Honey or the other people she had met. She wanted to tell everyone because it felt good to think about being there. However, she knew if she did they'd probably lock her away.

So, she kept quiet.

Chapter Fourteen

As Joy sat at her desk she drifted off in her thoughts once again. When she opened her eyes this time she was in a hospital bed. Michael was sleeping in a chair next to her bed. He was snoring softly with his head tipped back. Joy giggled a bit. He was a funny sight but also a comforting sight. She was happy to be back.

She looked to her right and there were several bouquets of flowers adorning her bedside. There were roses from Michael, a mixed bouquet from Fred, Carnations from Marge and Jack, and several other vases full of flowers from people all over the island. She was touched that everyone cared so much about her. Her eyes teared up a bit.

Just then, Michael rustled in the chair and groaned a bit. A nurse peeked in the door to check on her.

"Oh I see you're awake. I will get the doctor and let him know. How do you feel?" asked the nurse.

"I feel pretty good, a little nauseous. Is the baby....okay?" Joy asked.

"Oh, yes the baby is fine. You just need to take care of yourself and get plenty of rest. They started you on some prenatal vitamins. Your iron was really low," the nurse comforted her. "Do you need anything?"

"No, I'm good," Joy told her.

"Okay, here's the buzzer," the nurse told her as she handed the call switch to her. "If you need me push the little red button and I'll be back in a flash. The tv remote is here," she set the remote on the table next to Joy. Then the nurse left the room.

"Mmmm, was that the nurse?" Michael asked as he stretched awake.

"Yes, she said the baby is fine!" Joy said happily.

"I know. I'm just glad you're alright," Michael told her.

"Mom has been looking after Honey. I'm going to run home, shower and change my clothes. Would you like something from the house?"

"Maybe just some clean clothes and make up," Joy answered.

"Alright, I know you are in good hands here, but I won't be gone too long," said Michael.

He stood up, stretched, and walked over to the window. He pulled the curtain open to let some light in. Then he walked over to Joy and put his hand on her head caressing her hair. He leaned in and kissed her.

"I'll see you soon, Sweetheart," Michael told her.

"See you soon," she replied.

Joy was happy she was still pregnant in this alternate life. She didn't know if it was real but everything felt real and that's all that mattered. It was the life she had dreamed of, mostly. She started thinking about her parents and how they would never be Grandparents in the real world. She began to wonder about her parents in this alternate life.

Maybe her Mother and Father are still alive in this alternate life. She thought for a moment if they are then she can share this experience with them. She wondered if they would be the same as her real parents. She hadn't met anyone in this life that was the same as in her real life. Her pets weren't even the same. She wasn't worried about her pets anymore. She knew she could count on Julie in the real world. Michael and his parents seemed to be taking good care of Honey. If this was an alternate universe it wasn't like any movies she'd seen.

As she was deep in thought Dr. Lewis walked in. He seemed to be in a great mood today and he wasn't just carrying a clipboard. He brought in a bouquet of flowers.

"Good morning, lovely lady, I just saw your husband leave," said Dr. Lewis. "You gave us a scare."

"Dr. Lewis, are you sure the baby is alright? The nurse told me the baby is fine," Joy asked.

"Yes, the baby is fine and please call me Kurt. You always called me Kurt before," he smiled.

"Okay, Kurt," Joy said awkwardly.

"Joy, how are your memories coming along?" he asked.

"To be honest, I'm confused. I don't remember anything before washing up on shore the day David and Patricia pulled me out of the water. Please don't tell anyone else. I don't want to hurt Michael's feelings," Joy answered.

"Understood. Your secret is safe with me," he said in a serious tone. "In fact, I want you to be comfortable telling me anything. There will be no consequences, Joy. You and I go way back. We've always been good friends. I want you to feel safe, but more importantly I want to help you get better and I want you to remember," Dr. Lewis told her.

Joy suddenly did feel safe. She felt like he was being completely genuine with her and that she could trust him. Maybe this is what she felt back at the beach home when he came to visit. Maybe it wasn't a physical attraction but a deep friendship that they shared.

She wanted to tell someone about the real world and what she had been going through but she still wasn't ready to tell anyone in this universe. She didn't want to end up speaking to a psychiatrist here too. She wanted to keep this place perfect.

"Are those flowers for me," she gestured towards the bouquet in his hand.

"Oh yes, I think there is a vase in one of these cupboards," he said as he opened and closed several doors in search of a vase. "Ah! There, I found one."

Dr. Lewis pulled a large vase out of one of the hospital room cupboards and filled it with water. He carefully placed the flowers in the vase and set them next to Joy. Then he took special care to arranged them to look fuller.

"Now, as for your treatment, I want you to take the prenatal vitamins once a day. You need to get plenty of rest. You don't have to stay confined to a bed, but I don't

141

want you trying to walk Honey alone and no other strenuous work or lifting. If you need help with Honey there are plenty of people who can help you and I don't live far away. Just call me anytime if you need something or if anything is wrong," he told her. "We are going to observe you for a few more hours and probably release you this afternoon."

There was a loud commotion in the hallway. It sounded like a bunch of men stirring things up. She could hear indistinct voices get louder and clearer as they came closer to her room.

"No, only two visitors at a time!" a nurse said.

"But I want to see Joy!" said a male voice.

"Me too!" bellowed another man.

"The doctor is in there with her, so let me check before you just barge in!" another nurse told them.

"Well hurry up!" said yet a third man.

"Yeah! We wanna see our lil sis!" said the fourth voice.

The nurse knocked on the door, "Doctor, Joy has some visitors. Is it okay to send them in? There are four people here to see her."

Dr. Lewis looked at the nurse, "Step out and shut the door and tell them just a moment."

"Sure thing," said the nurse as she closed the door.

Dr. Lewis looked at Joy, "Do you remember anything about your brothers?"

Joy's eyes got wide, "My brothers?"

"Yes, brothers," he answered, " I guess that means no? Do you want to see your brothers?"

"Yes, of course I want to see my brothers, but will you stay? I didn't even know I had brothers. Do I have sisters? Do I have parents?" she asked.

Dr. Lewis looked at her sort of strange and laughed, "That's an odd question. Everyone has parents. Do you mean to ask if your parents are alive?"

"Yes, that's what I meant," Joy answered.

"You don't have any sisters," he told her.

Dr. Lewis sat down on the edge of Joy's bed so he could look her in the eyes. He reached out to hold her hand as if he were about to deliver bad news.

He took a deep breath and said, "Your mother died of cancer several years ago," he paused for a reaction.

Joy deflated and sighed in disappointment. "What about my dad?"

"Your dad left your mother when you were a child. You haven't seen him in many years. I'm sorry," the doctor told her.

Joy perked up, "But I have four brothers!" she smiled.

"That you do. The oldest and tallest one is Sam, then Ed has blonde hair about the same color as yours. There is no mistaking that Ed is your brother. The next one is Greg. He doesn't look like he is part of the family and he is the shortest. The youngest one is Henry. Henry is pretty quiet and shy ," said Dr. Lewis. "Are you ready for them to come in? They seem to be getting louder the longer we make them wait."

"Sure, let's do this," she smiled. She couldn't wait to see what her siblings looked like. She had always wanted siblings and now she had them.

The doctor opened the door, "Come on in guys."

"Sis!" yelled Sam.

"Joy!" shouted Ed.

"We're glad you're alright," said Greg.

The youngest one Henry didn't say anything. He just had tears in his eyes. He rushed over to the bed and hugged his sister.

"Guys, I have to ask you to be quiet. You are in a hospital and Joy is going to be fine, but she does need her rest. We don't want to get her too excited," Dr. Lewis told them.

"How did you find out I was in the hospital?" Joy asked them.

144

"Michael called me and I told the others," Sam explained.

"Did he tell you what happened?" Joy asked.

"Only that you're pregnant!" Ed tried to contain himself.

"I can't believe our lil' sis is having a baby," said Sam proudly.

"Do you know when the baby's coming?" asked Greg.

"No we haven't had a chance to discuss that yet," Dr. Lewis answered for Joy.

"Do *you* know when the baby is due?" Joy asked Dr. Lewis.

"You are about twelve weeks along," Dr. Lewis told her.

"I'll come stay on the island and help take care of you," Sam told her.

"That's sweet and I'd like that but Michael and Dr. ...I mean Kurt are taking good care of me. And Patricia and David are so helpful. I'm sure they will be excited to hear the news if Michael hasn't told them already. Besides, I'm sure you have a job?" said Joy.

"A job, silly sis' you know I've been a stay at home dad," Sam answered.

"Yes, and his wife Amber is a lawyer," Kurt added quickly.

"Yes, Amber. How is she?" asked Joy. "Don't you need to be home to take care of your children?"

"Joy, are you feeling okay? You know Carrie is away at college and Sean is old enough to take care of himself..." Sam answered with a puzzled look.

"I'm okay," Joy answered.

"Sam, it's probably her medication. It makes her sleepy," Kurt covered for her quickly.

Sam didn't appear to believe Kurt, he felt something wasn't quite right. "Still I'm going to come stay in your spare room and keep an eye on you for a few days," Sam told Joy.

"Really, Sam, it's not necessary. Honestly I'm just fine. Now tell me how everyone is doing," Joy said.

Ed shoved Sam aside and stepped up, "Well, I'll tell ya how I'm doing! I got that promotion I was hoping to get. Laura quit her job and she's opening that scrap booking business at home. She's so excited. The kids are healthy and that's all that matters."

"Oh Ed, I'm so happy for you. Congratulations," Joy told him.

"And look at you," Ed smiled. "You are simply glowing!"

"Ann picked out this gift for the baby," Greg handed Joy a package wrapped in soft pink and blue colors. It was tied with a transparent lacy yellow ribbon.

"Thank you, should I open it now?" Joy asked.

"Yes, please do," Greg answered.

Joy carefully untied the lacy yellow ribbon and removed it from the package. Then she picked gently at the tape.

"Oh just rip it!" said Ed.

"You know Joy likes to take her time opening presents. Leave her be," Greg told Ed.

Joy smiled at them and looked back down at the package. She pulled the wrapping paper off and folded it neatly. She slowly lifted the cover off the box and pulled back the tissue paper inside the box. She pulled out a unisex sleeper. It was covered in tiny little geese. It was so tiny and when she looked at the sleeper things became very real to her.

Joy got tears in her eyes, "I love it, Greg. Tell Ann thank you, I love it."

Henry just stood there smiling at Joy quietly.

"And what about you, Henry? What have you been up to?" Joy asked.

"Not much," said Henry.

"How's your new job, Henry?" asked Kurt prompting him for more conversation.

"It's okay, I guess," said Henry.

"New job? I'm having trouble recalling what exactly you do?" prodded Joy.

Sam tilted his head and furrowed his brow as he placed his hand to his chin. Yet he said nothing. It was still bothering him that Joy was having difficulty with her memory.

"I got a job on the fishing boats," Henry replied.

"Henry has always been a man of few words," Kurt said.

Joy suddenly felt a dizzy spell coming on, "Ohhh.."she said as her head started spinning.

"Joy!" shouted Sam.

"I need you to all leave the room," said Kurt firmly.

The last thing Joy saw was Kurt ushering her four brothers out of the room as everything went black.

Chapter Fifteen

This time Joy didn't wake up at her desk. This hadn't happened before. She woke up in her bed at home. Fitch was curled up at her feet and it was the middle of the day. She had never had a black out like this in the real world. The only place she had memory gaps or lost time was on Goose Island. This brought new fears and questions to mind.

She thought maybe she was just dreaming all of it. Maybe she had dreamed part of it. Honestly she just didn't know what to think. She still felt a little dizzy so she stayed in bed with Fitch for a bit. Her cell phone was on the night stand so she sent a text message to Julie.

"Hey, do you know anything about how I got from work to my home and who brought me here?"

"Yes." was the simple reply from Julie.

Just then Julie opened Joy's bedroom door and peeked her head inside. She was smiling and holding a tray of food.

"Eric and I brought you home. You had a dizzy spell at work again. Has the counselor shed any light on what is going on?" Julie asked.
"No. I have an appointment for them to examine my brain," Joy smirked. "I'll be there an entire day. I'm gonna end up losing my job. I don't have enough vacation time or sick days for all of this," Joy said in a distressed voice.

"Don't worry, your boss actually understands and everything will be fine,"Julie answered. "Joy, you don't realize how much they need you."

Joy stared out the window, and she looked preoccupied by her thoughts.

Julie could tell something else was bothering her.

"What else is on your mind?" Julie asked.

"I just have a bad feeling about this counselor. I can't put my finger on it, but something is telling me not to go," Joy confessed.

"Oh I'm sure it's just nerves. It will be fine, you'll see," Julie tried to console her with her words.

"Did you happen to feed my fish and Fitch?" asked Joy.

"It was the first thing I did when I got here. Your pets will always be well cared for. So tell me, have you been there again? Is there anything else to tell?" Julie prodded.

"On Goose Island I'm still pregnant. Here I'm just getting fat and depressed," Joy answered.

"Really? Anything else to tell?" Julie questioned her.

"Yes, I have four brothers on Goose Island. My mother died of cancer and my father left us when I was a just a child," Joy explained.

"Four brothers, how interesting. What do they look like?" Julie asked.

Joy went on and explained everything about her last visit to the island. Julie hung on every word as if it were some type of soap opera.

"What really bothers me is this time when I came back it was different," Joy went on.

"How so?" Julie asked.

"I blacked out at work and woke up here instead of at my desk," Joy said.

"What do you think that means?" Julie asked curiously.

"I don't know. I think it means something has changed," Joy told her.

"You really don't remember Eric and I picking you up at work and bringing you home?" Julie asked.

"No, I have absolutely no recollection of that at all," Joy answered.

"You were talking. I mean, you weren't carrying on intellectual conversations or anything, but when we asked you a question, you answered. It was a bit like talking to a drunk. You don't have a drinking problem, do you?" Julie asked.

"Of course not. Besides if I were drinking heavily don't you think you would smell it on my breath?" Joy asked.

"I'm sorry, you're right," Julie apologized.

"This is just all so weird," Joy sighed.
"I wish there were something I could do to help," Julie told her.

"I wish I could just be one place or the other. I have no control over this thing. And you *are* helping. I think I can get up now. I should probably go shower or something. How long was I out?" Joy asked.

"Nearly a good solid day, you passed out yesterday. You were sort of in and out of it all last night and this morning. Now I can see you have a clear head. You are speaking in complete sentences," Julie chuckled.

"Do you find this funny?" Joy asked.

"Aww Joy, you know I love you. Lighten up," Julie said attempting to diffuse Joy. "I didn't mean to hurt your feelings."

"I know, but if you were going through what I'm going through you wouldn't laugh about it at all," Joy told her.

"I'm sorry. Well, since you are feeling better I'm going to leave. I have a lot to do. Eric drove your car home and it's parked in your garage. But maybe you shouldn't be driving?" Julie explained.

Joy didn't like the thought of not being able to drive but she knew Julie was right. She thought about how she might black out while driving and possibly kill or injure someone else. However, her stubbornness and desire for freedom out-weighed all of that. So, she lashed out at Julie for suggesting such a thing.

"How dare you tell me what to do! I'm tired of people telling me what to do and treating me like a door mat!" Joy yelled irrationally.

"I don't treat you like a door mat. I know you are going through a lot but don't take this out on me," Julie told her.

Joy realized she had just hurt her best friend, "I'm sorry. I shouldn't have blamed you. It's just that if life wasn't bad enough before....you know, losing my parents and being stuck in this dead end thankless job.." she started apologizing.

"I know. You don't need to say anymore. Just remember, Joy, none of us have perfect lives. We all go through *stuff*. That's just how it is. I realize your *stuff* is quite different than my *stuff*. Very different than ANYONE'S stuff. But I'm here for you, always," Julie told her and hugged her.

"Yes, I guess I've been a little selfish. I haven't been there for you lately," Joy said.

"Don't worry about me right now. I'm doing alright. When we get you through whatever this thing is, you can be there for me when I need you to be," Julie smiled.

Julie let her know that she'd check back in on her later and left. Joy got out of bed and looked around her house. She noticed things were collecting dust and there were dirty dishes in the sink. The laundry hamper was spilling over. She realized she hadn't been doing her basic housekeeping. Joy took a shower and began cleaning up her home. She decided that even if she couldn't control this thing that was happening, she could at least take control of something. She knew that doing these little things would make her feel like her life had some order in it.

A few days later Joy arrived at the office of Dr. Vanderstein. She made sure she arrived a few minutes early. Joy was always on time if not early for her appointments. She flipped through the magazines in the waiting room pretending to read. She couldn't think about anything but this appointment and what would or could happen.

Her stomach was upset and she had vomited earlier this morning. The smells of the office were making her feel sick now. She was beginning to feel ignorant about even setting up this appointment. Her entire body was screaming at her to cancel the appointment and go home.

"You can go back now," the receptionist chimed.

Joy set the magazine on the table, grabbed her purse and walked into the doctor's office.

"How are you today, Joy?" asked Dr. Vanderstein.

"A little nervous," she confessed, although she was more than a *little* nervous.

"Well, just relax. Miss Smith will conduct the testing in another room," he explained.

He walked her in and introduced Joy to a woman with brown hair and a baby face. She looked like she hadn't even graduated high school.

"This is Miss Smith, Miss Smith this is Joy," said Dr. Vanderstein and he left the room closing the door behind him.

"You can call me Pearl," said Miss Smith.

"Okay," said Joy.

"Have you ever had testing like this done before," asked Pearl.

"No," Joy answered.

Pearl looked over Joy's record, "I see they pulled your school background. It shows you were an honor student and received an academic scholarship to the University."

"Is that normal for them to do a background check on someone getting one of these tests?" asked Joy.

"It's pretty common. I see it a lot," answered Pearl. "No previous disorders," she went on reading.

Joy sat silently and anxiously.

Pearl read on, "recent weight gain, depression..."

"I'm not depressed," said Joy.

"Okay," said Pearl as she continued reading aloud, "laceration?"

"Yes, it's no big deal. I accidentally cut my hand cleaning up some broken glass. It's all healed now except for this scar," Joy explained as she pointed to her scar.

"Both of your parents are recently deceased, is that correct?" Pearl asked.

"Yes," answered Joy.

"...and it says you work in an office, right?" Pearl continued.

"That's right," Joy was feeling impatient. She had been asked these questions several times before and completed them on several forms. It was becoming quite redundant.

"Just bare with me. We'll begin shortly. I just want to make sure all of this information is accurate," stated Pearl.

"I understand," Joy told her.

"It says you've reported having dizzy spells and passed out at work, but you deny using alcohol, tobacco, and drugs," Pearl read on.

"That's correct," Joy answered.

"We will be doing a neuro-psychological evaluation today," Pearl spoke into a small personal recording device. "This will include behavior observation and a mental status exam. The procedures will be as follows. The Wechsler Adult Intelligence Scale, Wide Range Achievement Test, Boston Naming Test, Controlled Oral Word Association, Conners Continuous Auditory Test of Attention, Achenbach Adult Behavior Checklist,

Minnesota Multiphasic Personality Inventory, Mental Status Exam, Clinical Interview...."

About that time Joy began losing interest and thinking about Goose Island.

All of the big words and Pearls talking was boring her. Then Pearl broke Joy's concentration.

"Joy?" Pearl said.

"What?" asked Joy.

"I asked if you are ready to begin?" Pearl told her.

"Oh sure," she answered.

Pearl grabbed a large binder and set it on the table in front of her. Then she reached down and grabbed a bag and poured it out on the table. Out fell several plastic triangle shapes. She opened the binder to the first page. It showed two triangles arranged in a specific way.

Pearl pointed to the page, "See I want you to arrange the triangles in the same way as pictured here just like this."

Pearl took the triangles and moved them into position as an example. Joy nodded. Pearl turned the page and there were three triangles on that page.

"Okay it's your turn," Pearl told her.

Joy felt like she was in elementary school. She thought to herself, "You've got to be kidding me."

Each time Pearl turned the page there were more triangles and more complicated pictures. Joy completed each one quickly and easily. They worked on the triangle test for several minutes. Then they moved onto the next test. Joy was finding all of the tests simplistic and childlike. She was beginning to think this was just a huge waste of time.

After lunch Joy was beginning to feel tired. She didn't eat much since she still had an upset stomach. Pearl took her into another room with a desk and a computer.

"Here, you sit here and you'll answer several questions. This will take a while but answer them as quickly as you can. Don't think about them too much just type the first thing that comes to mind," Pearl explained and left the room.

Joy began the test answering yes or no questions. As she would read them she thought many of the questions could be taken good or bad either way depending on your mindset. It almost felt like a trap. Some questions were easy such as "Do you love your father?" or "Do you love your mother?". Other questions seemed like they were loaded questions and Joy began to over analyze. She was growing weary and wondering why they had not given her this test early in the morning. She would have preferred taking the easy tests this afternoon, especially since she was feeling drained.

She felt ill and dizzy again. So she put her elbows on the desk and rested her eyes in the palms of her hands. Then everything went black.

Chapter Sixteen

Joy woke up. She was back in the hospital again on Goose Island, "Oh no," she thought. "What if I'm acting like I'm drunk and barely functioning during that evaluation?! They will think I'm on drugs or something. I need to get back there right now. But how?"

Joy tried concentrating, she tried going to sleep, but nothing was working. She was at a point that she realized she had no control of when she went home and when she was on the island.

Dr. Lewis walked into the room with her chart and a grimacing look on his face. He walked over and stood next to Joy.

"I'm glad to see you're awake. I have some troubling news. We ran some blood work and found a toxin in your system. It would explain the dizzy spells, your passing out, and the memory loss," he explained.

"Then you can fix it?" Joy asked.

"The problem is we don't know how the toxin got into your system," he explained. "We need to find the source...where you are ingesting it or how you are coming into contact with it before..." he stopped.

"Before what?" she asked.

"...before it kills the baby and you," Dr. Lewis told her in solemn voice.

"What is it?" Joy asked nervously.

"Echinoix 5," he answered.

"I don't know what that is. Where does it come from?" Joy asked.

"It's a pharmaceutical drug that can be obtained only with a prescription," Dr. Lewis answered. "The good news is we've flushed most of it out of your system. Your husband is here and can drive you home. Michael wants to take you home to keep an eye on you. I would like you to stay here for better monitoring."

"I think I'd like to go home. I rest better there," Joy told him. Joy really wanted to try to get back to sleep so she could get back to the evaluation in the real world before someone walked in on her.

"I want you to keep a diary of everything you eat and touch, even who visits. Keep track if you are getting sicker or if you feel better. If you get any worse I want you back here immediately!" Dr. Lewis told her.

"I promise," said Joy.

"I'm serious, this is nothing to mess around with. You just had trace doses in your blood but if you keep coming in contact with it, then you could die. I will need to research the drug further. I'm going to talk to Fred and find out if anyone is getting that prescription from his pharmacy. Maybe someone is not disposing of it correctly. If it was in our water system then everyone would be sick. I really wish you'd consider staying here just in case this is intentional," he told her.

"You mean you think someone could have poisoned me?" Joy asked.

"I doubt it because everyone here loves you, but I don't want to rule anything out. Don't tell anyone about this, not even Michael," Dr. Lewis told her.

This was a frightening thought for Joy. It still wasn't enough to keep her in the hospital. She really wanted to leave as soon as possible so she could get back to the real world. She couldn't think about anything else right now.

Michael walked in shortly after the doctor and Joy finished talking. He had a bag of clothes for her and wheelchair to take her out to the car. He set the bag at the foot of the bed.

"Here ya go, clean clothes," Michael said to Joy.

Joy grabbed the bag of clothes and the men walked out into the hall to let her change.

"So, doc, how is she?" asked Michael.

"To be honest I'm very concerned. I really wish she would stay here for observation. You'll need to keep a very close eye on her and if she gets worse, I mean the slightest thing, then bring her back immediately," Kurt told him.

Michael looked really worried, "Her brothers are hanging around for a few days, so they will help out."

"That's comforting to hear," said Kurt. "I'll stop by and check on her too."

"That won't be necessary," Michael appeared to be a little jealous. "I'm sure you have enough to do. You shouldn't be giving all of this extra time and attention to my wife. I'm sure there are plenty of people on this island that need your help."

"Michael, she's my friend and it's no trouble at all. In fact, it's my duty to check on her," Kurt responded.

Joy came out of the room in her clean clothes, "I'm ready!"

"Oh sweetheart you need to sit down," Michael told her as he wheeled the chair over to her.

Joy sat down in the chair, "Really I'm quite capable of walking."

Michael began to wheel her down the hall towards the door and Dr. Lewis called out to her, "Remember to call me if you need anything!"

"I will!" she shouted back.

When Michael and Joy arrived at the house Honey jumped up in the front window barking. Honey was excited to see Joy. Joy started to open the car door and get out.

"Wait! Let me get that," Michael told her. He jumped out of the car and ran around to the other side to open the door.

"All of this attention is great, but really I feel okay," Joy told him.

"Look, I'm not going to let anything happen to you so just let me take care of you," Michael told her.

Michael helped Joy walk up to the house and when they got inside she wanted to go upstairs and lie down in the bedroom. Honey was wagging her tail and following them all the way, she wanted to play.

"No, Honey go lay down. I'll take you for a walk later," Michael told Honey.

When they entered the bedroom Michael walked Joy over to the bed and pulled the covers back to let her lie down. He pulled her nightgown out of the closet and helped her change into her sleepwear. He gently tucked her in and gave her a kiss on the cheek.

"Do you want anything?" he asked.

"No, I just want to go to sleep," she told him. "Maybe you should take Honey for a walk right now."

"But what about you? What if something happens? I can't leave you here alone," he fretted.

"I'm just going to sleep and the phone is on the nightstand if there is an emergency," she told Michael. "Really, don't worry."

"Okay, but I'm not taking her for a long walk," Michael said. "I'll only be gone a few minutes."

Michael pulled the curtains shut to make the room darker and kissed Joy again. He grabbed Honey's leash and took her out of the room. They went down the stairs and Joy heard the front door open and shut.

Joy laid in bed staring at the ceiling. She was thinking about the real world and her evaluation. That was just keeping her awake. In fact, it was stressing her out. She was wide awake. She covered her head to make it darker, but that didn't work either. Then she started thinking about what Kurt told her. She couldn't imagine why someone would want to kill her. Everyone she met was nice to her and cared about her. She decided that idea was just ridiculous. She thought maybe if she had some warm milk it would help.

Joy pushed back the covers and threw her legs over the side of the bed. She put her feet in her slippers. She felt a little dizzy but she walked toward the door. She carefully went down the stairs holding the handrail just in case she lost her balance.

When she got into the kitchen she searched through the cupboards and found a microwavable cup. She walked over to the refrigerator and was going to grab the milk but started feeling hungry when she saw the food.

"No, I need warm milk so I can sleep," she said to herself.

She grabbed the milk and poured it into the cup and put the cup in the microwave. While the milk was warming she noticed a cookie jar on the counter in the shape of a bunny rabbit. She wondered if there were any cookies inside. She thought one or two cookies with the milk would be quite delicious and settle her stomach.

Joy took the lid off the cookie jar and there were homemade chocolate chip cookies inside. She grabbed two of them and began eating one of them. The microwave buzzer went off and she eagerly opened the microwave. She pulled the cup out quickly but it was hot and it burned the palm of her hand enough that she jumped. When she jumped she dropped the cookies and the cup and the warm milk spilled on the counter and the floor. At this moment Joy slipped in the milk and lost her balance. She didn't fall but when she lost her balance she reached for the counter to steady herself. There just happen to be a sharp knife on the counter and it sliced into her forearm.

Blood was spilling out and it swirled into the milk that was on the floor and the counter. Joy became woozy and passed out.

"Grab her! We must sedate her immediately!" yelled Dr. Vanderstein. "What happened here Miss Smith!?"

"I don't know! She was taking the test, I left her alone in the room like we do with everyone," Miss Smith said in a panic.

"She's a danger to herself, we must sedate her and have her committed immediately! What did she cut herself with?" yelled the doctor.

"I don't know, maybe something on the desk," Miss Smith answered as she struggled with the doctor to hold Joy still.

"Nurse! Nurse! Get the first aid kit we need to bandage this wound and stop the bleeding. And bring me that shot!" yelled Dr. Vanderstein.

Joy felt dizzy, her arm was pulsing with pain, and everything was blurry. It was her worst nightmare come true. She was screaming because she was in a tremendous amount of pain but she was also screaming because she didn't want them to sedate her and lock her away.

"I didn't hurt myself!" Joy screamed. It was the last thing she could say clearly before she felt the needle enter her arm.

Just then the doctor administered the sedative and Joy went limp. The nurse helped him stop the bleeding and bandage her arm.

"Good the cut isn't that deep. I think we've stopped the bleeding but she'll need a few stitches. Miss Smith, call an ambulance and we'll have them tend to this before we admit her to the psych facility," said Dr. Vanderstein.

After Miss Smith called the ambulance she began looking around the room for what Joy could have used to make the cut.

"I don't see anything, doctor," said Miss Smith.

"Look, right here. This paper spindle. It's sharp and she could have easily sliced her arm open on this. See, it even has blood on it," the doctor told her.

Miss Smith looked at the spindle and Joy's blood was on it but strangely enough the tip was clean. She knew that couldn't be how Joy was cut.

"Don't touch it, in fact don't touch anything else. The police will need to file a report. Nurse, tell the receptionist to cancel all of my appointments for the rest of the day. Actually, for the next few days. We'll need some pros in here to clean up all of this blood when the police are done," said Dr. Vanderstein.

Joy lay on the floor muttering, "...didn't...I didn't...no, I didn't" until she passed out completely.

Chapter Seventeen

Joy woke up in a white room with no television, no monitors, and she was wearing paper scrubs. Her arm was bandaged quite well. They had taken her purse, her cell phone, and all of her personal belongings. Joy was angry.

The door opened and a woman walked in, "Hi Joy, I'm Dr. Kane. I just need to ask you a few questions if you feel up to it."

"Whatever it takes to get me out of here as soon as possible," Joy told her.

"Can you tell me about what happened in the room?" asked Dr. Kane.

"I didn't hurt myself," Joy snapped at her.

"You can see how it would appear you did, right?" asked the doctor.

Joy just glared at her.

"When you are ready to talk about it, then maybe we can talk about getting you out of here," said Dr. Kane.

"Where's my stuff? I want my cell phone," Joy demanded.

"Your things are secured in a locker and we don't allow cell phones in the room because you may get a text message that would cause you to be depressed, angry, or feel desperation. We want you to remain as calm as possible so you can get better," the doctor explained.

"I FEEL ANGRY NOW! I don't belong here!" Joy insisted.

"Calm down," the doctor told her.

"CALM DOWN? I live alone, my pets are alone! I need to call my friend Julie!" Joy yelled.

"Julie?" Dr. Kane jotted her name down on a pad, "Do you know her number or is it on your paperwork?"

"She's my contact person," Joy told her in a calmer voice.

"I will go check on that and come back to let you know what is going on, okay?" said Dr. Kane.

Joy sat with her knees by her chest and her arms wrapped around her knees. She kept her head downward angrily and then she simply nodded. Dr. Kane got up and left the room. Minutes felt like hours. About twenty minutes later a nurse walked in and handed Joy some pills.

"Here take these," the nurse told her.

"What are they?" Joy asked.

"Your doctor ordered them, just take them and we'll both feel better," the nurse said in a mean tone of voice.

"Where's Dr. Kane? She was calling my friend," Joy asked.

"Take your pills and I'll go find out," the nurse told her.

Joy pretended to swallow the pills and the nurse left the room. Thirty minutes later Dr. Kane came back to the room.

"We got Julie on the phone. She knows you are here. You can't have any visitors the first two days. After that, if approved by our staff, then Julie can come visit," Dr. Kane explained. "She told us to tell you the pets are fine."

"I'll lose my job for sure," Joy grunted.

"It's my understanding you are on family medical leave for now," Dr. Kane explained. "So don't worry about your job. Concentrate on feeling better."

"You can't keep me here," Joy insisted.

"Here's what is going to happen," Dr. Kane informed her. "You will be assessed by several doctors and a social worker. Our team will decide if it is safe to

173

send you home. At this point, it appears that you cut yourself so it doesn't bode well for you."

Joy listened intently and the more Dr. Kane explained how she could be released the more she worried. She was certain the longer she stayed the more evidence they would find against her sanity. She stressed she would never get out of there. And as much as she loathed her job, she would rather be at work right now. Her job had been her prison for many years, but this was worse. She had lost all of her freedom.

"This is not a quick process." Dr. Kane went on. "There are quite a few people participating in this process. It is really involved and there are a lot of steps you need to go through."

"Do you have a time frame of when you would expect me to be able to leave?" Joy asked.

"That all depends upon you. The average stay here is about a week or less. In your case, I can't say yet," Dr. Kane told her. "If you are released we will also have to determine what type of outpatient treatment you require."

"And what if I just leave?" asked Joy.

"You can't. The doctor has ordered you to be confined and assessed. You are a potential danger to yourself and others. You need to understand we are doing this for your safety and the safety of others," Dr. Kane answered.

"But I haven't hurt anyone," Joy told her.

"You will be here for a while, so just get comfortable and follow instructions. If you do as you're told and things go well, then you could be out sooner rather than later," said Dr. Kane.

"I just want to go home. Can't you see *this* isn't good for me?" Joy cried.

"Look you've been through a traumatic event. The tragic loss of both your parents has effected you in an extraordinary way. Joy, you attempted suicide.." Dr. Kane started saying.

"I DIDN'T TRY TO KILL MYSELF! I DIDN'T EVEN TRY TO HURT MYSELF!!!" Joy screamed as tears ran down her cheeks. "Why won't anyone listen to me?"

"I can see you are still in denial," Dr. Kane told her. "We will be moving you into your room in a few hours. I will check on that and have the nurse let you know when that will be."

"My room?" Joy asked.

"Yes, this isn't your room. This is just an observation room. Your room will be more like a hotel room. They will give you menus to order your food. We

175

have classes here that are therapeutic. We want you to participate in as many of these as you are comfortable with," Dr. Kane answered.

Joy was a ball of rage inside, but she knew she needed to calm down, act normal and get out. Aside from the pain from her arm and the rage inside, she was experiencing some abdominal pain. She was not very good at hiding her physical pain.

"Did the nurse come give you your pain pills?" asked Dr. Kane.

"Yes, she did," answered Joy.

"It appears you are in pain, are you?" asked Dr. Kane.

"A little," answered Joy.

"I'd say it's more than a little from your body language. On a scale of one to ten with ten being the greatest what level of pain are you experiencing?" asked Dr. Kane.

"About a six maybe," Joy answered.

"I'll be right back," Dr. Kane told her.

The doctor got up and walked out of the room. Joy got out of the bed and walked to the door. She tried to open it, but the door was locked from the outside. There was nothing in the room, no windows, just the bed. Joy got down on the floor and looked under the bed, but found nothing. The door knob rattled so Joy climbed back onto the bed as quick as she could.

Dr. Kane walked in concealing something in her hand. She walked over to the bed and put her hands on Joy's arms.

"Just relax," she said as she quickly stuck a needle into Joy's arm. "I suspected you didn't take your meds. I reviewed the video and saw that you concealed them. So we can do this the hard way or the easy way. You aren't off to a good start."

Joy felt sleepy, "Did you give me something besides pain medicine?" she asked.

"Just a little something to help you relax," said Dr. Kane.

Joy fell asleep and Dr. Kane left the room.

Joy began dreaming and she had good dreams. She dreamed she was on the island and that she was surrounded by her family and friends. As the dream progressed her pregnancy progressed and she dreamed of her baby shower. As it continued she had a beautiful baby girl. Then suddenly the sky grew dark and ominous as bellowing clouds rolled in. The clouds grew faces and arms and the wind picked up. Leaves were blowing around and the wind was trying to take her baby. Joy held on as tight as she could but a cloud reached down and ripped the baby from her arms. Then Joy woke up.

Joy sat up in bed she was in a strange room. She didn't know if she was on the island or in the real world. The room was rather dull and plain. The bed was dressed in a yellow flowered blanket. The curtains matched the blanket. There wasn't much furniture in the room and there was no phone and no television. Then someone knocked on the door.

"Hello, Joy? Can I come in?" asked Julie.

"YES!" Joy answered in delight.

Julie rushed over to the bed and hugged Joy so tightly, "I'm so sorry you're in here. They said you tried to kill yourself, but I just can't believe that."

"No, I didn't, you know me too well," said Joy. "Are they treating you well?" asked Julie.

"They keep me sleeping mostly. When I don't take my medicine they inject me. When I'm coherent they prod me with questions. I've seen about five different doctors, I think. How long have I been here?" Joy asked.

"I was told today is the first day they would allow you to have visitors. You've been here two days," Julie told her.

"How's Fitch and my fish?" she asked.

"Fitch and the fish are fine. I think they miss you but I'm taking good care of them. I even slept there one night to keep them company," Julie told her.

"You're a good friend. I knew I could trust you," Joy told her.

Julie felt guilty that she even suggested to Dr. Paememor that Joy might have mental issues. She blamed herself for Joy's situation. So she just forced a smile on her face.

"Does Nicole know I'm here?" Joy asked.

"I just got a chance to tell her yesterday. She will be here to visit you tomorrow," Julie answered.

"Has anyone given you any idea when I will get to go home?" Joy asked.

"Not yet, I will see what I can find out," Julie answered.

A nurse popped her head into the room, "Hello, Joy? It's time for therapy painting," she said to Joy. "I'll have to ask you to leave. You can come back between three to six today or visit her tomorrow," she told Julie.

"But I just got here..." Julie told her.

"And I was told the classes were optional. I want to visit my friend. I don't feel like painting," Joy told the nurse.

"Well, visiting hours have just ended for the morning, so she'll have to leave. If you don't want to paint you can sit in your room," the nurse answered.

"I'll come back and see you later today. It might be good for you to get out of this room," Julie told her.

"Yes, I guess I will go paint," Joy told the nurse.

"Okay, come with me," the nurse told her.

The nurse ushered Julie and Joy into the hall. Joy hugged Julie and the nurse walked Joy down the hall to the left. Julie headed the other way toward the exit, but realized she left her purse in Joy's room. The door was still cracked open so Julie went in and grabbed her purse. She looked around the room feeling very guilty. She reached in her purse and pulled out a cell phone she had picked up at the store. She knew it was against the rules but left it under Joy's pillow with a note that read "Talk soon! Love Julie".

As Julie walked out the door to leave Pearl was coming in the door and they nearly bumped into each other.

"Oh, excuse me," said Julie.

"Is this Joy's room?" asked Pearl.

"Yes, who are you?" asked Julie.

"Who are you?" asked Pearl.

"I'm Julie, Joy's best friend," she answered.

"Oh thank goodness. You are the Julie on Joy's contact list?" Pearl asked.

"Yes, why?" Julie asked.

"I was coming up to talk to Joy about what happened. I'm the one who was giving her the evaluation test the day Dr. Vanderstein claims Joy tried to commit suicide," Pearl answered.

"I think Joy has enough doctors to talk to right now. Anyhow she is down at the therapeutic art class," Julie told Pearl.

"No, you don't understand. I spoke with the police and there is no evidence that Joy attempted suicide. I had reviewed her profile and the testing she completed. Things just didn't add up." Pearl explained.

"What do you mean?" Julie asked.

"I mean I think Dr. Vanderstein is wrong. He claimed that Joy cut herself on the paper spindle, but there was no blood on the tip. There was blood on the base of the spindle just none at all on the tip. If that was the item she used then there would have to be something on the sharp part. There was nothing else sharp in the room. So, how could Joy have done this?" Pearl asked.

"What do you think happened?" asked Julie.

"Your friend Joy is very intelligent and she doesn't have the personality of a person who would do something like this. I don't know why she is working in an office. She's really working beneath her means and ability. Maybe she lacks confidence. Joy has the brains and talent to be anything, do anything. I don't know what happened, but she didn't do this to herself," Pearl told her.

"Okay, so how do we get her out of here?" Julie asked frantically.

"It's not that easy. Dr. Vanderstein signed the order that put her in here. I don't have the authority to get her released. And just the information I have by itself won't do it. We need one of the doctor's here on our side," Pearl added.

Pearl noticed a staff member staring at her and Julie. It made her uncomfortable. She grabbed Julie by the arm and began to lead her away.

"We had better go," Pearl told her as they walked down the hall toward the exit.

"Here's my card and my cell phone number is on it."

Julie jotted down her phone number on a piece of paper, "Here's mine. Call me if you have any more ideas or can help further."

"I will," answered Pearl. They kept walking together outside as they talked.

"I'm coming back to see Joy this afternoon, I will let her know you were here and what you've found out," Julie said. "And thanks."

"It's my pleasure. I got into this profession to help people, not harm them," Pearl answered.

"You seem like a really good person and Joy needs good people in her life," Julie told her.

"Who doesn't?" said Pearl.

Pearl walked up to a car, "This is me. So, we'll be in touch."

"Okay, talk soon!" said Julie.

Chapter Eighteen

Meanwhile, Joy finished her painting in her therapy class. She painted a picture of the wildlife sanctuary that Michael took her to see. She painted the little ducks and had all of the colorful flowers and trees in the painting.

"Oh my, you are a natural artist, Joy!" the nurse told her.

"I guess it does look pretty good," said Joy.

"No, I mean I haven't seen *anyone* in here make a painting as beautiful as yours...ever. You've got some talent," said the nurse.

"Really, you think so?" Joy asked. "...you're just saying that to make me feel better."

"Joy, I know that *some* people in here will tell you what you want to hear. They do it to build your self esteem and make you happy. But I am telling you the gospel truth. I"ll bet if you took your painting to an art gallery they would buy it," the nurse answered.

"I think you are telling me the truth," Joy smiled.

"I absolutely love it," said the nurse.

"Then I want you to have it, Eleanor," Joy told her as she read her name tag.

"I can't..." said Eleanor.

"I insist. Please take it," said Joy.

"Have you seen this place before?" asked Eleanor.

"Yes, I've been there," Joy answered.

"Where is it? It's so lovely I'd love to go," said Eleanor.

Joy stammered a bit, "I- I went there a long time ago. I was very young and don't remember where it was. I'm sorry."

"Oh well, that's okay. At least I'll have the painting," Eleanor said with a smile.

Another nurse walked up, "It's time to go back to your room, Joy."

"See you later, Joy," said Eleanor.

"See you later," said Joy.

The other nurse walked Joy back to her room. Even though Joy thought some of the people were nice there, she still wanted to leave. She was making mental notes of an escape route if the opportunity presented itself.

"Here we are," said the nurse. "Make sure you fill out your meal card. Someone will be back to pick it up soon."

The nurse left the room. Joy sat on her bed and sighed. She scooted back on the bed, bumped her pillow, and it fell on the floor. She saw the note Julie left and was elated to see the cell phone.

"I knew I could trust you, Julie," she thought to herself.

The first thing she did was text Julie a thank you message. Joy was discreet about using the phone since she knew they may have cameras in the room to keep an eye on her. She had picked up her pillow and placed it back on the bed. She climbed into bed and kept the phone under the covers while she sent text messages back and forth to Julie.

Julie sent her a text message back, "I have some good news, but I will tell you when I get there in thirty minutes."

Joy was able to get on the internet using the cell phone. She was thinking about Echinoix 5 and was concerned it could be in her system in the real world. She began searching it on the internet and couldn't find it. She heard a noise by the door.

A nurse walked into the room, "Do you have your dinner card filled out?" she asked.

"Oh, sorry no," Joy said as she shoved the phone under the blanket.

"What were you doing?" the nurse asked.

"Nothing, just thinking," Joy answered. She quickly grabbed the food card and a pen. She filled out the card in a hurry and handed it off quickly to the nurse.

"Here ya go!" Joy smiled.

"You seem to be in a better mood?" the nurse observed.

"I am. Maybe the painting helped," Joy answered.

A short time later Julie arrived on time as promised. She walked in the room grinning ear to ear. Joy ran over and hugged her.

"Thank you, thank you, thank you so much!" Joy whispered.

"No problem,"Julie replied. "So, do you want to hear the good news?"

"Yes!" said Joy.

"Now don't get too excited, but I promise it's good. When I was leaving I met Pearl from Dr. Vanderstein's office," Julie told Joy.

"How is that good?" Joy asked impatiently.

"Let me finish…," Julie continued. "Pearl is on your side. She reviewed your file, and by the way, said you are really really smart and should be like a rocket scientist or something."

Joy rolled her eyes and looked at Julie with skepticism, but waited to hear what she had to say.

"Anyhow, she said your profile didn't fit that of someone who would try to kill themselves. She also said that the police investigated and couldn't find anything that you would have used to cut yourself. Dr. Vanderstein thought you used the paper spindle but Pearl said there was no blood on the tip. It was the only sharp item in the room! So this is all good news," said Julie.

"So, there is a but, right?" asked Joy.

"Yes, we need to get the staff here on board to get you released," Julie explained.

"I wonder if there was a video from that day," Joy told Julie.

"I will find out. I have Pearl's phone number," Julie said.

"That could be good or bad depending on what is on that video, if there is one," Joy said.

"What do you mean?" asked Julie.

"What if there is a video and it just shows a cut appear on my arm? Then what? Do they hand me over to scientists? Or what if I'm acting like I'm drunk as you described?" Joy asked.

"Well, don't worry I'll get on that. If there is a video I think we can trust Pearl to help. If the video will hurt your situation I'm sure Pearl will be cooperative in getting rid of it," Julie told Joy.

"How can you be so sure you can trust Pearl?" asked Joy.

"It was more of a feeling, but she stuck her neck out to come see you today," said Joy.

The next day, Dr. Kane came to see Joy for another assessment. She walked in with her clipboard.

"Good morning Joy, how are you today?" asked Dr. Kane.

"I'm pretty good. In fact, I'm quite happy I have some news for you," Joy told her.

"Your nurse said you were in better spirits after painting yesterday. What is this news you have?" asked Dr. Kane.

"I have proof I didn't try to kill myself," Joy smiled.

"You have proof? Where?" asked Dr. Kane with doubt.

"Well, I don't *have it* here. The police found evidence or maybe I should say *no evidence* that I attempted suicide. The only sharp item in the room didn't have blood on it," Joy told her.

"Who told you this?" asked Dr. Kane.

"My friend," Joy answered.

"Well, leave the diagnosis to the professionals. You won't leave until *we* approve it. And if there was nothing sharp in the room then how did your arm get a laceration?" asked Dr. Kane in a condescending tone.

Joy thought she better change the subject since this conversation was headed in the wrong direction.

"Dr. Kane, I have a question," Joy stated.

"Yes?" she responded.

"Can you tell me what Echinoix 5 is?" asked Joy.

"I can't say that I can. I've never heard of it. Why do you ask?" Dr. Kane asked curiously.

Joy played dumb, "I thought it was the name of a medicine you gave me. Maybe I heard a nurse say it or something."

Dr. Kane jotted down on her clipboard, "Echinoix 5 is that what you said? I will check with the pharmacy."

"Did they check my blood for toxins when they did my blood work?" Joy asked.

Dr. Kane looked at the chart, "I don't see anything out of the ordinary. Toxins would have been picked up in this blood work. None were found. You are asking a lot of unusual questions today, Joy."

"Maybe I just had some weird dreams or something. My memory has been a little messed up since I've been here. It's hard to know what day it is and if I dreamed something or it actually happened," Joy answered.

"That makes sense. People tend to get a little confused in here if they sleep a lot as you have," Dr. Kane answered as she continued writing.

Then Joy jumped a little and made a little noise like she was startled.

"What is it, Joy?" asked Dr. Kane.

"I'm sorry. It's nothing I think it's just a little gas," she blushed.

"Okay, well I'm done here today. When I come back I will hopefully have a suitable answer for you regarding Echinoix 5. I see you have group therapy today. You are not required to talk during this session but you are required to sit in and listen. Then later we have the craft room open and other classes available. Right now you are scheduled to go have some physical therapy. We need to keep you active. Physical activity keeps the mind healthy," Dr. Kane told her. Then she looked at the clock and said, "Your physical therapist should be here in about ten minutes."

Dr. Kane got up and left the room. Joy thought about the island and what might be happening there. But she was still more concerned about her real life and how to get released from the hospital.

Later that day, Nicole stopped by during visiting hours. When she walked in she almost didn't recognize Joy. Since Joy was not wearing make up and her hair was done up nice she looked very different. Also Joy had gained several pounds since she last saw Nicole.

"Hi, Joy. How are you?" Nicole asked.

"Hi, I'm about as good as can be expected considering the circumstances. Did Julie tell you everything?" Joy asked.

"She did. She also mentioned Pearl and her thoughts," Nicole answered.

"You look skeptical," said Joy.

"Well, you are in here and I'm sure it's for a good reason. I mean these people know what they are doing. Julie said you have seen several doctors. I'm sure when you are ready they will release you," Nicole told her.

"I'm ready now. You just don't believe me," said Joy. "I know it's a difficult thing to understand and harder to believe, but what is it going to take to prove to you I'm telling the truth?" asked Joy.

"I'm sure you are telling me what is true to you. However, what is real and what is fantasy are two completely different things," Nicole answered.

"So, even with Pearl and the police backing me up you don't believe me?" asked Joy.

"It's not that I don't believe you. I can believe that maybe something happened in that room that you can't explain and you were injured. I can believe that everything you are telling me you believe to be true. But to believe that you are somehow traveling to another world or place in some magical way, well, that's what I'm having trouble with," Nicole explained.

"I wish you could," Joy told her.

"I'm trying to keep an open mind, but it just seems impossible," Nicole told her.

"Anything is possible," Nicole replied.

"Have you been to Goose Island since you have been in here?" Nicole asked.

"No, I don't seem to have any control over that," Joy told her.

"Do you know what medicines they have you on?" Nicole asked.

"I'm so in and out of it from the meds that most of the time I don't know if I'm coming or going. I have no idea what day or time it is and if they told me the names of the meds I wouldn't remember," Joy answered.

"Maybe the medicine is helping. But I am concerned about your weight gain," Nicole told her.

"Yeah, tell me about it. They put me on a special diet to help me drop the extra pounds I've gained," Joy explained.

"That's good," Nicole seemed relieved.

"How are you doing?" Joy asked.

"My Mom is sick. That's why I haven't been around much. Thank God Julie has been so helpful. I'm sorry I haven't been able to be here for you more," said Nicole in a gloomy tone.

"Oh, I'm sorry is she bad?" asked Joy.

"She's in the hospital right now...we are...hopeful," Nicole answered.

"Tell her I wish I could come visit and I hope she gets well soon," Joy told Nicole.

"I will," she replied. "I'm going to see her after I'm done here."

"Well, you go and be with your mom. You belong with her," Joy said to Nicole.

"But.." Nicole started to say.

"But nothing, your mom is your family. I'm fine. Anyway Julie is doing a great job keeping an eye on things," Joy said.

"Joy, you are family," Nicole told her and hugged her before she left.

Joy has been in the psych facility for a few weeks now and she is growing impatient. She has had several doctors in to speak with her and still they keep delaying her release. She is beginning to think they are keeping her there for her insurance money. Even with the special diet she continues to gain weight. Joy is pacing in her room. Dr. Kane knocks and walks in.

"How are you today, Joy?" asked Dr. Kane.

"I'd be happier if you could tell me when you will release me," Joy answered. "You said the average stay here is about a week. I've been here several weeks. I'm gaining weight and I could swear I felt something move inside me. Maybe you should do another pregnancy test!"

"We told you that you aren't pregnant. Dr. Paememor ran that test already but if you want to pay out of your pocket for another one, then we can send someone in for that tomorrow," Dr. Kane said with contempt.

"Where have you been anyhow?! This is the first time I've seen you in weeks! What about Echinoix 5? I asked you about that weeks ago and you never have answered that question!" Joy was aggitated.

"Echinoix 5, there is no such thing. It doesn't exist," Dr. Kane told her. "As for where I've been...I was on vacation, not that it's any of your business."

"Vacation! I'm rotting in here and getting worse and you are on vacation! I'm telling you something is wrong! Why don't you listen?" Joy demanded.

"You should *listen* to you doctors and trust what we tell you. We didn't go to school for years and earn that degree for nothing," Dr. Kane recoiled.

"I don't know why you have such a big chip on your shoulder! I may be *just* a patient to you in a psych ward, but *you are employed by me* and my insurance, so you better just listen!" Joy snapped back.

Dr. Kane got up and left the room abruptly. She came back armed with a syringe and two male nurses.

"I can see you need to calm down," said Dr. Kane. "Maybe you'll be more cooperative and respectful next time we talk."

She gestured for the male nurses to hold Joy down while she injected her with the syringe.

"Noooo!" Joy screamed as her voice faded into nothingness.

Joy began to blink as light entered her eyes. The room was blurry, but this time she was back in the hospital on Goose Island. Patricia was in the room adjusting her flowers as she woke up. Joy moaned and Patricia turned around.

"Oh dear! You gave us such a scare. You have to stop doing that," Patricia told her. "I'll go get Dr. Lewis. He's just down the hall."

Patricia ran out of the room and Joy looked at her belly. Her baby bump had grown a considerable amount and she felt the baby kick. Joy smiled and rubbed her belly.

Chapter Nineteen

Joy looked down at her bandaged arm. She was hooked up to machines and an IV. Her arm had nearly healed, but she was pale and in a lot of pain. Patricia came rushing back to the room with Dr. Lewis in tow. They were nearly tripping over each other to get into the room.

"Joy! Thank God, you've been out of it for weeks!" said Dr. Lewis.

"Kurt," Joy replied weakly.

"Take it easy. How do you feel?" he asked.

"My arm feels better. My stomach hurts," Joy answered.

"Okay, I'm going to check your vitals again and we'll give a listen to the baby's heartbeat," he told her. "Patricia, would you go call Michael and let him know she's awake?"

"Yes, doctor," Patricia answered and left the room.

"What's wrong with me?" Joy asked.

"Quickly, can you tell me what happened to you at the house before Michael gets here? Did he – did he hurt you?" Kurt asked.

"No, no," she said softly. "He went for a walk with Honey. I went downstairs to get a snack. I wanted some warm milk and I made it too hot, I dropped it. I slipped and there was a knife on the counter. I somehow landed on it," Joy told him.

"Okay, he said he found you that way. I just wanted to make sure," he explained. "We need to get to the bottom of what's going on but I suspect someone is poisoning you,"he told her. "Since you've been back in the hospital your toxin levels of Echinoix 5 have risen. We are keeping track of visitors on the sign in sheet, but you've had a lot. I think we may need to isolate you to protect you."

"What about the hospital security camera?" Joy asked.

"The what? Why would a hospital need a security camera?" Kurt asked.

Joy thought, "Oh must be something else they don't do here."

"Could you set up a secret camera in my room and record or monitor people that way?" Joy asked.

"That's a good idea, Joy. I'll get a technician to set something up. But in the meantime we need to keep visitors out, including your husband," Kurt answered.

"I feel so faint and my stomach hurts bad," Joy told him.

Dr. Lewis put on his stethoscope and placed it on Joy's tummy. Then he listened to Joy's heart. He took her temperature and blood pressure.

"I can still hear the baby's heartbeat," he told her. "Hang in there. I see you need your IV bag changed. I'll do it myself. I've been changing the bag and administering your medicines myself since I noticed your toxin level was on the rise. Unfortunately, there's been no change, even with my extra precautions."

"Kurt, I appreciate everything you are doing. I think I need to confide in you and I hope you will believe me," Joy said.

Just then Michael walked in, "Joy! I'm so glad to see you're awake. I will never forgive myself for leaving you to walk Honey."

"No, don't blame yourself," she labored to talk in a quiet voice. "I told you to take Honey for a walk and it was my decision to go downstairs and get a glass of milk. You have no reason to feel at fault."

"Joy, don't try to talk! Just rest," said Michael.

"Yes, Michael is right. You need to rest," Dr. Lewis agreed. "Michael, I feel it's best if Joy doesn't have any visitors for the next several days. This includes you."

"What?! Why?" asked Michael.

"I can explain later," the doctor told him.

"No! Explain now!" Michael insisted.

Just then Joy let out a moan and Michael grabbed her hand. Dr. Lewis was changing the IV bag while Joy and Michael held hands and gazed into each others eyes. Dr. Lewis left the room to go grab some supplies. Michael leaned over and kissed Joy.

Just then Joy let out a scream of pain, "Aahhhhh! My abdomen feels like it's on fire! Aaaahhhhh! Somethings wrong!" she screamed again. She began to sweat profusely.

Michael grabbed a damp towel and wiped off her forehead, "doctor!!!" he yelled.

Dr. Lewis and his team came rushing into the room, "What did you do to her?!" he asked as he shoved Michael aside.

The monitors were going crazy. Buzzers and beeping saturated the room.

"Michael, you need to leave now!" yelled Dr. Lewis.

"I WON'T!" Michael yelled.

The doctor began giving his team orders, "Joy I'm going to check your cervix."

Michael had to be pulled out of the room by security. The doctor pulled back the blanket and the sheets were soaked in blood. He couldn't find the baby's heartbeat this time.

"Joy, you're losing the baby," the doctor told her.

"No," she whispered faintly.

"Stay with us! Stay with us!" he shouted. "We have to get her into the operating room NOW!"

Joy was in and out of it, and several hours passed with the team working on her and the baby frantically. Joy was declining.

The last thing Joy heard was, "the baby's gone."

Then Joy woke up in intense pain screaming in a similar situation back in the psych facility. Only this time Julie was there to witness what was happening. Pearl came rushing back into the room with a team of doctors right behind her. There was blood everywhere and she knew now the doctors were wrong! She was miscarrying this baby too. They carted her off to an operating room.

"Don't leave me, Julie! I don't trust them!" Joy screamed as they wheeled her away.

"I'm here, Joy!" she yelled.

Nicole walked in just in time to see them wheeling Joy away covered in blood. She heard Joy's screams from down the hall and rushed to see what was happening. There was a trail of blood that followed Joy.

"What happened to Joy?!" Nicole asked Julie.

"The home pregnancy test was right and her doctor was wrong. Joy was pregnant. They took her to the operating room to see if they can save the baby and get Joy stabilized," Julie answered.

"How can that be?! What kind of doctors can't read a pregnancy test?!" Nicole asked.

"It's not likely that baby will live with all of the anti-psychotic drugs they were giving her. If it does, it could have some serious birth defects," Pearl told them. "I wish I could have done something sooner."

"We need to get Joy a lawyer and get her out of here," Nicole told them.

"It's my fault she's here," Julie told them as tears poured down her face.

"How so?" asked Nicole.

"I told her family doctor she might have mental issues," Julie sobbed.

"It's not your fault. The doctors misdiagnosed her. How many doctors did she see? Five, six? And no one figured out she was pregnant!?" Nicole told her.

"She's right," said Pearl. "The doctors are to blame for this. I'm probably going to get fired for saying this, but Joy has got a big malpractice suit."

"Right now we have to pray that Joy will live through this!" said Julie.

"You go pray, I'm going to find her a lawyer," said Nicole.

"I came down here today to tell her that the medical doctor on the staff here noted in her file that her injury didn't appear to be self inflicted. He noted that on the first day she was admitted. He also noted that the injury appeared to be caused from a serrated knife and there was no way it was done with a paper spindle," Pearl informed them.

"So, do you know what Joy has been telling us about how she was injured?" asked Nicole.

"Yes, I've had some conversations with Julie and I have promised to keep it secret," said Pearl.

"And what do you think about her Goose Island?" asked Nicole.

"My logical mind tells me that it can't be, but in science we discover new things every day. The evidence is beginning to build up in Joy's favor that this is really happening," Pearl answered.

"We don't need evidence of that to prove malpractice and get her discharged. What do we do to help her next if she continues to experience these visits?" asked Nicole.

"I don't know. This is all uncharted territory. We just need to be there for her and be supportive," said Pearl. "I have a friend that's a doctor, but he is open minded. He believes in things like the paranormal and has studied quantum physics. I think he may be able to help her."

"So, you believe Joy now?" Julie asked Nicole.

"It's getting pretty hard to remain skeptical," Nicole replied.

Three days later, Julie walked Joy into the door of her own home. Fitch came over rubbing up against the legs of her long lost friend. Joy eased down onto her couch. Fitch yowled until Joy sat down. Then Fitch jumped into Joy's lap and began purring. Joy held her cat and enjoyed the sights and smells of her home that she had missed.

"Oh I missed you so much, Fitch," said Joy as she hugged her cat.

"Nicole, Eric and I will take turns coming over to take care of you until you are completely recovered," Julie told her.

"Thank you, so much," said Joy.

"I still blame myself. I had no right saying anything to your doctor," Julie confessed.

"No, you did what you thought was right. Besides, you know those doctors treated me unfairly," said Joy. "You were the only one that even remotely believed what I was saying. Even Nicole took a lot of convincing and she's still not 100% on board."

"Nicole got the attorney for you that was able to get you released. She said he has sent a subpoena for all of your medical records for the malpractice. Pearl said she would testify on your behalf if necessary. The attorney said it's likely they will settle this thing pretty fast to keep from causing you more stress," Julie told her.

"Nicole is burying her feelings in work. I appreciate all that you, Nicole and Pearl have done to help," Joy told her.

"Speaking of work, your boss is anxiously awaiting your return. They really do need you there. Those flowers on the table are from your employer," Julie told her.

"Well, it's nice to feel appreciated," Joy sighed.

"Do you think it's over?" asked Julie.

"Do I think what is over?" Joy asked.

"I mean, do you think you will visit Goose Island again?" asked Julie.

"You know I don't know how it happens. I'm guessing it's not over yet," Joy answered.

"Maybe Pearl and her friend can help," Julie said.

"I don't know, maybe. But if I do go back, I have to find out who poisoned me and why," Joy told her. "It seems that Goose Island is not the perfect place I thought it was."

Julie sat down next to Joy and put her arm around her. Joy looked around and remembered things she had forgotten and felt free. Even with the loss of her baby, the feeling of freedom outweighed her mournfulness. Freedom was the best feeling she had experienced in weeks.

Watch for the next book!
Coming in 2019…

Made in the USA
Lexington, KY
06 November 2019